Breck: Encouraged to Love

The Barnabas Chronicles
Book 13

By

Ronna M. Bacon

Psalm 32:8

Paraphrase from NKJV

God will instruct us and teach us in the path that we should walk. He will guide under the care of His eye.

Table of Contents

Chapter 1

Standing at his office window, a mug of fresh coffee in his hand, Breck Curran stared out at the falling leaves. He had just returned from a two-week vacation that he had desperately needed, heading up to a northern park in Ontario, to a favourite camping spot. He felt refreshed, he thought, but he still had concerns about the men of the Barnabas Foundation, the twelve of whom had undergone what they termed as adventures but in fact, had been life and death situations. He sighed as he rubbed at his dark auburn hair.

Breck turned finally, heading for his desk and then searching his schedule. This afternoon, he realized, he was due to meet with the landscaping contractor about the new playground and gardens that the Barnabas Foundation was planning at the local shelter. He was looking forward to that. Until then, Breck had paperwork to look over and complete. Being second in command under his friend, Barnabas Carey, at the Foundation was work he usually enjoyed. At the moment, though, he was restless. Even the vacation had not calmed that feeling.

Parking his truck near the shelter, he waved at the older couple who ran it for the Foundation. Cadee, one of the men's wives, had seen her parents leave the mission field that they loved and then take over the shelter at Barnabas' request. They were loved by all the inhabitants.

—

7

Breck moved around the building, heading for the activity that he could see. He stopped, waiting for the equipment to move past him, and then headed towards the contractor.

"Ben Deakin, it's good to be working with you." Breck's hand was out to shake the older man's.

"Breck! It is good. I hear tell that you had a vacation. Hope you enjoyed it."

"I did. Way up north, camping in a park. Peaceful. I think every doctor should prescribe that for patients."

Ben laughed. "I agree. We don't get to camp much now, not when we are so busy, but we used to." He nodded towards the grounds. "We're just getting started as you can see. These are the plans that the board approved."

The two men studied the blueprints and then walked the boundary, Breck asking all the right questions, Ben thought. He knows his stuff, this young man. If he didn't have work with the Foundation, I'd hire him.

Nevin approached his father, pulling off his hard hat and wiping at his face. Even though it was late into the fall, the sun was warm that day.

"Dad? We're about ready to start the dig. Any further instructions?"

Ben turned, watching the small skid steer as it moved into place. "No, I think we're ready. Go for it. You two always enjoy playing in the dirt."

—

Nevin grinned. "That we do." He turned and ran for the equipment, hopping up to speak with the operator, before he was off and to the side, watching as it was driven forward, and the first scoop of dirt moved.

Breck watched closely before he frowned. He turned, finding Ben back at his truck, just pocketing his phone.

"Ben?"

Ben looked up at Breck's call and then moved his way. "What's up, Breck?"

"I don't like something there. Can we stop for a moment?"

"We can." Ben waved off the equipment operator and then walked forward with Breck. Breck bent over and then straightened up.

"It's what I thought. Bones."

"Bones?" Ben took a look and paled. "We have never found bones before on any dig." He sighed, waving Nevin over. "Nevin, call off the dig. We just found human bones."

Nevin stopped short, not sure of what his father was saying. "Bones?"

"Bones. Get Neasa and get back to the truck. The equipment stays where it is."

Breck walked back towards Ben after speaking with the responding officers. He sighed. This was not how he had planned his first day back. He had spoken

—

with Barnabas, who was on his way to the site. Now, how did he explain it to Ben?

"Breck? How long?" Ben was waiting for him.

"They don't know. They have to wait for a medical examiner to come in. The techs are working around that. This will put you behind."

"Not a problem. We'll work to get it started at least this fall." Ben turned. "It's those two I'm worried about."

"Who?" Breck squinted, the motion narrowing his dark brown eyes.

"Nevin and Neasa. Neasa is the one who was on the equipment."

"Neasa? I don't know that I've met Neasa."

"No, I don't think that you have. She's been away all summer, working on her grandfather's farm, helping him out. She's back now." Ben moved towards his children. "I'll introduce you, although she does say that she has seen you around church."

"More than likely. I seem to get more and more involved. I need to pull back some."

"And you will. Neasa? This is Breck Curran. He's from the Foundation."

Neasa Deakin looked up, way up, she thought, as she smiled at Breck. He's tall and good looking. Likely taken too. She sighed to herself.

"Hi. It's good to meet you. Sorry about this."

———

"Sorry? It's not your fault. You didn't bury a body there, did you?" Breck grinned as she frowned at him, studying the long golden blond hair in a braid and the cornflower blue eyes.

"Certainly not. Dad, we can still lay out what we need to do, can't we? That way, we'll be ready to get back to work once the site is released."

"That we can. How be you and Breck take a walk around the perimeter? I think that should be okay." Ben frowned for a moment and then shrugged. "See what we need to do."

Breck waited for Neasa to refuse but she headed off, making him almost run to catch up with her. He walked beside her, his attention on the activity around the dig.

"This has never happened before." Neasa finally stopped, watching her father. "I don't know what Dad will do."

"He'll wait for clearance and then start again. He seemed to think that you could get a lot done this fall yet."

"We can if the weather holds." She turned suddenly, her hand shading her eyes. "Do you hear that?"

"Hear what?" Breck spun. "An ATV. There shouldn't be one around her." He grabbed for her hand, pulling her with him, heading for a small shed near the shelter.

Only, they never made it in time. The large ATV was in their path without warning and then heading

---

directly for them. Breck could hear shouts around him as he dove out of the way, Neasa wrapped in his arms. Struck a glancing blow, he rolled, his head hitting hard on the packed dirt, and then lay still, Neasa not moving either. The ATV slowed and then sped off, even as patrol officers raced for their vehicles and followed. Ben gave a shout and ran for his daughter, Nevin racing from where he had stood watching the activity.

Ben's hand shook as he knelt beside the pair, reaching out for Neasa. Nevin was beside him, a hand on his shoulder.

"Dad?"

"She's alive, son." He reached for Breck. "So is Breck, but they're hurt." He stood back as patrol officers moved in and then the paramedics. "We'll follow them."

Ben turned as he felt a hand on his shoulder again, to find Barnabas Carey standing there.

"Ben? What happened?"

"They were walking around the plot, trying to determine what they could do, when an ATV appeared. It ran them down." Ben turned back as he watched the activity around the pair. "Who?"

"Likely related to the find." Barnabas was torn. He felt that he needed to stay with his life-long friend, Breck, but he also needed to talk to the investigators. He sighed. "You're heading in? I'll follow as soon as I can."

———

Chapter 2

Late that night, or rather early the next morning, Breck shifted uncomfortably in his hospital bed, pulling at the plastic bracelet around his wrist. He wanted out of there, not having to lay there and listen to the squeak of rubber-soled shoes as the nurses moved around. He wanted to find the person responsible for running him down. But, more importantly, he wanted to find Neasa Deakin and make sure for himself that she was not harmed. Barnabas had been around, checking up on him. He had reassured Breck that she was okay and in a room just down the hall from him. That didn't suit Breck at all. He needed to see for himself that she was fine.

He looked up as he heard a whisper of sound and squinted through the low lighting, his headache pounding. He watched as the form at the door looked behind itself and then moved towards him.

"Breck?" Neasa stood beside his bed, a large bandage on her cheek. "How are you? I escaped from the nurse. She'll be looking for me shortly."

Breck stared at her. "You escaped your nurse? And you're dressed. Planning to escape the hospital as well? Take me with you?"

"Breck!" Neasa shook a finger at him. "That's not what I asked."

"I have a headache if I must answer, as well as assorted bumps and bruises. How are you?" Breck watched her eyes, seeing a slight flicker of pain in them. "And don't tell me that you are fine. I know you're hurting."

"I am, Breck, but not as much as I could. You took the brunt of it." Neasa sounded frustrated.

"Of course I would. That's what we do for ladies." Breck sat up in bed. "Are you leaving the hospital?"

"I was hoping to. Nevin left transportation for me." She turned away and then back. "Why? You planning on leaving as well?"

"If I can catch a ride with you."

Neasa grinned. "You can. I'll tell Sue that we're leaving. She said that she had our discharge papers for the morning. As far as I'm concerned, it's morning."

"It is. Give me five minutes and I'll be with you." Breck waited until she had left the room and then rushed to dress, staring at the dirt stains on his clothing. Just how close was it, Lord? Just how close?

He watched from the hallway as Neasa headed his way, waving his paperwork, trying to walk as quietly as she could. But he could see her limping. Lord, who was that person after? Me or Neasa? And did I just start an adventure like my friends?

Neasa pointed to the stairs and then shoved open the door.

"This will take us down to the Emergency Department and then we can make our great escape." She grinned at him.

"You think this is an adventure, do you?" Breck followed her down the stairs, stifling his groans at the pain.

"I do. I've heard of these kinds of adventures. Always wanted one." She walked through the opening door to the outside, waving at the security guard as she did so.

"Twelve of my friends have had them. You don't want one." Breck paused, looking around for her vehicle. "Where did your brother leave your car?"

"Car?" Neasa began to laugh. "This way." She paused beside a nice shiny brown and chrome motorcycle. "This is our transportation. But I can call for a cab if you would prefer that."

Breck stared at her and then the bike, walking around it, a soft whistle coming from him.

"Nice. I haven't ridden in years, even though I keep my license up to date." He grinned suddenly. "You driving?"

Neasa stared at him before her eyes narrowed. The lighting in the parking lot was just bright enough for her to see the mischief on his face.

"Of course." She looked around, suddenly shivering. "Can we leave? I don't feel safe."

"We can." Breck waited until she had seated herself before he climbed on behind her, taking the helmet he was handed and putting it on. He looked

---

down at his hands before he set them gently on her waist. It was not him, Breck thought, to do this to a lady, but he didn't have much choice. "Before we leave, can I pray?"

Neasa twisted to stare at him and then nodded. When he had finished, she looked at him. "Where do you want to go?"

"On a nice long ride with a beautiful lady?" He grinned again, knowing that he was flirting with her, not something he did either. "The Foundation building or wherever."

"I was heading for Dad's. I've been staying there since I came back. I hadn't settled into an apartment yet."

"Then, head there. I won't have you on the road on your own at this time of night."

"I've done it before." Neasa sounded disgruntled.

"You may have, but not from dropping me off. I refuse to let you."

Chapter 3

Barnabas stood the next morning, frowning at Breck's apartment door. He had talked to Breck the night before and Breck had been told to call him if he needed a ride home. That had not happened. He sighed. *Breck, where are you?* Barnabas rubbed at his head, suddenly exhausted. *We don't need Breck to disappear,* he thought.

Finally standing in his own office, Barnabas stared at his phone, scrolling through all his messages and then checking his email. Not a word from Breck. *That was not him,* he thought. He soon was immersed in his paperwork, looking up in surprise at the tap at his office door. Branigan and Brody, two of the men from the building, stood there.

"Barnabas, have you seen Breck? We were to meet with him today and he's not around." Brody sat in one of the chairs in front of the desk.

Barnabas leaned back in his own chair. "No, I haven't. Not since I saw him last night just as visiting hours ended. He was hoping to be home today."

"That's what we thought you'd say." Branigan leaned against the door frame. "So, where is he?"

Barnabas held up a finger as he dialed a number.

"Dan? It's Barnabas. How are you today?"

"I'm fine. Just heading in to pick up Neasa."

—

Barnabas could hear the house doors closing and the sound of Dan walking across the pavement.

"Barnabas, her bike's not here. I wonder if Nevin took it in for her."

"And if he did, she'd be home. Right?"

"Right. Hang on, let me call him. I'll call you right back."

Dan frantically dialed Nevin's number, only reaching his voice mail. "Nevin? It's Dad. Did you take Neasa her bike? We can't find her or Breck."

Barnabas was on his feet, not waiting for Dan to call him back, Branigan and Brody right behind him.

"Your truck?" Brody's question halted Barnabas for a moment before he nodded.

"My truck. Let's move, fellows. I don't like this."

"We don't either."

The three carefully watched the sides of the roads as they drove back in to the hospital, running for the doors and then the stairs inside the building.

Barnabas stared at the charge nurse before he ran his hand through his hair, frustration in his moves.

"He left? During the night?"

"That's what Sue said. Their discharge papers were all ready. She watched Neasa and Breck head down for the stairs. Is there a problem?"

"There is. Neither of them is answering their phones." Barnabas moved away to take a call. "Dan?"

"No sign of her bike. I can't raise Nevin, but if he's running equipment, he can't hear me. I'm heading towards that job site."

"I'm at the hospital. Neasa and Breck left real early this morning."

"They did? That's not like her." Dan sighed. "But then, she's become a lot more independent and withdrawn with us. She's not always opening up to us with where she's going."

"No? Did something happen to trigger that?"

"We're not sure. Even Nevin has commented on that." Dan reached to start his truck. "I'll be in touch as soon as I talk to Nevin. In the meanwhile, I guess we call the police?"

"I'll call it in." Barnabas turned to face the two other men. "No sign of Neasa at home. Dan says her motorbike is gone."

"Motorbike?" Brody shook his head. "Does Breck know she has one?"

"I would suspect so, by now." Barnabas had walked away and then returned shortly. "Dan called. Nevin dropped off her bike here late last night. He had talked to her briefly. She was planning on heading to Dan's."

"And if Breck knew, then he would have asked her for a ride. And he would not have let her bring him to the building." Branigan's hand slapped at the brick wall he was standing beside, frustrated. "So, where are they?"

"I spoke with Will, eventually. He's going to have a couple of patrol cars search for them." Barnabas stood for a moment before he headed back down the stairs. "We'll search as well. Where are the others?"

"At work. Other than for Burnie and he had a conference call with his publisher today." Branigan fastened his seat belt. "Let's pray, fellows. Breck needs that."

Chapter 4

Three days had gone by and still no sign of Breck or Neasa. Dan had been out, worried about his daughter, but he could provide little help. Nevin had been around as much as he could, seeking information but also company as he tried to find his sister. The men of the building had searched the roads surrounding the Foundation lands, had been through the town, talked to the people on the street, talked to Cadee's parents, and still had found no sign of Breck or Neasa.

Barnabas looked up that day and rose, walking towards his father, Bruce.

"Dad? I wasn't expecting you here this week. Mom with you?"

"She is. Anna and she headed into town, to see what they could do. Anna talked to Dan this morning. He's not even able to work, and he needs to. I talked to him last night. The authorities have released the land by the shelter and they want to get started on it. But they don't have the heart to do that. I'm talking with the board. Given the circumstances, we may delay that work until the spring."

"Likely a good idea. I am sure that the police will want to go back there at some point. I talked to Dallas last night. Will asked him to get involved."

"Good. He's got a head on his shoulders." Bruce poured them both a mug of coffee before he leant back against the counter in the kitchenette, one hand resting on it. "What are your feelings, son?"

"I don't know, Dad. This is not Breck. He stays in touch unless he's away on vacation." Barnabas paced. "Where are they?"

"God knows, son. The prayer chains are working. Breck is too well-liked by everyone not to have that happen."

"I know, Dad. We have had our differences over the years, but nothing really major. We've always been able to talk things through. Or at least pray over them." The younger man stood staring out the window across the lands. "They haven't found Neasa's bike yet, either."

"So, someone has hidden it. It would not be either one of them. I don't think that Breck has any enemies, not that we know of. Have you talked to his parents?"

"I wish I could. They're off somewhere in another province, with no phone service. He had told me that they expected to be gone for a couple of months. If I need to, I'll have Dallas track them down."

Barnabas reached for the phone on his belt, pulling it out and staring at it.

"That's Breck's ring." He tapped the phone, bringing up the text messages. "Oh, man! Where are you, Breck? And what did you do?"

Bruce was at his son's side, studying the picture that had arrived. "He's in rough shape, son. Any way to determine where he is?"

"I'm not sure, Dad. Look. Behind him. What do you see?"

"A shadow of a cross? Where is that?"

"I don't know." Barnabas sent the photo on to Dallas. "Maybe Dallas or his team can work wonders." Barnabas began to pace, his eyes studying the picture. "I know, Dad. It's near the shelter. That old rundown church that we were looking at buying to turn into apartments. Do you think?" His voice died away, even as his father reached for his arm and pulled him with him.

"Who's around today?"

"Brady was. Brandon. Blair. Which one?"

"All of them. Brady needs to bring his supplies. We may need his medical experience. It won't be the first time we've used his paramedic skills."

The three men stared at Barnabas for a moment before Brady ran for the well-stocked infirmary in the building and then for Blair's truck, following Barnabas as he shot out of the driveway.

Bruce watched closely as they neared the church, finally pointing to a parking lot.

"In there, I think, son. We can walk in from here. It's only a couple of minutes, I would think."

"I think so, Dad." Barnabas checked his phone. "No word from Dallas. We're on our own, I guess." He slipped from the truck, meeting the other three. "Dad, pray for us. We'll need that."

"Absolutely, son."

The five walked quickly towards the building, their eyes searching but not seeing anyone, which they found strange. There were always people in the area.

"This is strange." Blair kept his voice low. "Where is everyone?"

"It's like they were scared away. What did Breck get involved in?" Brandon stopped, his eyes on the church. "Do we go in or do we wait?"

"I'm going in." Barnabas stood for a moment, his heart raised in prayer. "Brandon, stay here. Send a message if anyone shows up."

The four men ran quickly for the building, ducking inside and then stopping to listen. They exchanged puzzled glances before they moved forward, around the debris and broken pews, towards the front of the church. Brady's hand went up, as he tilted his head.

"Do you hear that?"

"Hear what?" Bruce didn't hear anything. Not at first. "A female voice."

They moved forward cautiously, stopping outside a closed door, their eyes on one another before Barnabas reached for the doorknob and turned it slowly, the door opening inch by inch under his touch. He stepped through, the other three behind him, as he searched the room, finding startled blue eyes on him before his own eyes dropped to the floor.

"Breck!"

Chapter 5

Brady was past Barnabas, dropping to his knees beside Breck before he looked up at the lady.

"Are you okay?" His voice was low.

"I am. But Breck isn't. Please? Will you help him?"

"We can. We need to get you up and out of here." Barnabas reached for her, finding her drawing back.

"I can't." She lifted an arm, showing them the shackle that held her imprisoned, near to Breck but not near enough to touch him. "They did this to me. To make me stay. I couldn't stop them." Her eyes filled with tears as she looked over at Breck. "He tried to stop them, to make them leave me alone. They did that to him."

Blair had followed the chain to the floor as Neasa had spoken, a muttered word or two coming from him. Bruce was at his side, a pocketknife out as he dug at the eye-bolt that held the chain, Blair tugging at it to free it.

"Neasa? Come with me." Bruce had her on her feet, the chain gathered in his hand. "They'll bring Breck."

Neasa refused to move, watching as Brady and Barnabas spoke quietly and then lifted Breck to his feet and over Brady's shoulders. She finally moved at the tug on her arm, trying to watch where she was going at the same time as she watched Breck. Bruce finally just shook his head and swept her up into his arms, almost running for the door, the men following closely.

Brandon took one look and then ran for the trucks, the key fobs in his hands clicking to unlock the doors.

"Who goes where?" He paused as he studied first Breck and then Neasa.

"Breck and Neasa in the back. Brady, you're with them. Dad?"

"I'm in front. Blair? Brandon?"

"We'll follow. Doc's on duty today."

"The Lord was working things out there." Barnabas pulled out his phone, tossing it to his father as he sped off. "Answer that please, Dad."

"Bruce? You have Barnabas' phone?" Dallas' voice held puzzlement.

"I do. We have Breck and Neasa. We're heading to the hospital with them. They were in that old abandoned church near the shelter."

"The old church? We searched it, two days ago. They were there?" Dallas' attention went to the traffic ahead of him. "Just a moment, Bruce. I am heading back your way, once I can get out of traffic." His hands-free device disconnected, leaving him muttering at it.

Bruce dropped the phone into the cup holder on the centre console before he glanced to the back seat. "Brady?"

Brady shook his head. "Sorry, Bruce. I'm not sure. He's hurting, I know that, but from where all? I can't do a proper assessment."

Bruce's eyes turned to Neasa, finding her watching Breck intently. "Neasa? May I call you that?" He gave a half-smile as she nodded without looking at him. "Did they hurt you?"

"No, just the shackle. We tried to escape. That's when they did that. They hid my motorbike somewhere. I don't know where though." She looked up, anger sparking briefly. "Why?"

"That's what we'll work on. We'll get you two seen to first." Bruce turned his head to watch the hospital appear. "Emergency doors, son?"

"You've got it, Dad." Barnabas had regressed to his teens with his language and phrases, his concern on Breck. He parked and then was out, helping Brady as he moved Breck to a stretcher and then reaching for Neasa, only to find that she wasn't there. "Where'd she go?"

Bruce grinned at his son. "You didn't see her moves? She was around you and ahead of the stretcher before I could stop her. Blair and Brandon were right behind her."

Barnabas stared at his father and then the closed doors. "I never saw her. Let me park, Dad, and then we'll head in."

"No, son. Let me. You'll be needed, I think." Bruce watched as his son nodded and then moved quickly to enter the department, before he shook his head, his eyes raised to the sky. *Dear Lord, I don't know what's going on, but You do. Heal our boy, dear Lord.*

Doc finally came to find Barnabas, stopping as he saw all the men from the building there. He had been told that they were and that the ladies had gathered in the chapel. He shook his head. *Lord, this boy is going to go through something, something bad. Protect him and his lady.* He turned for a moment to stare behind him, a slight smile on his face. Neasa had refused to move from Breck's side, insisting that she needed to be there. That he had been hurt because of her.

Barnabas was on his feet, moving towards Doc, a frown on his face, hearing the steps behind him as the men gathered there,

"Doc?"

"He's a fortunate man, Barnabas. Lots of bruisings. Defensive wounds on his hands and arms. No broken bones. He's been for imaging and so far, we don't see any internal bleeding. He's rousing, now that we've been able to start an IV and rehydrate him."

"Thank God. You'll be keeping in overnight?"

"I would like to, but I don't see that happening. I'll take him back to our place. I'm off tomorrow so that should work."

"And Neasa?" Bruce spoke up, worry for the young lady on his face.

———

"Neasa? The lady who won't leave Breck? What's the story there?" Doc searched the faces, seeing understanding on some but curiosity on others.

"Neasa? She was with him when they were run down four days ago it is now." Barnabas didn't catch the speculative glance Doc sent his way. "She's okay?"

"She is. She just won't leave him. And he's clinging tight to her hand. We can't get him to release it."

Chapter 6

Breck raised his head from the pillow during the night, squinting as he glanced around in the low light. At least not the hospital this time, he thought, but I'm not sure where I am. His head was pounding, harder than it had been, and he sought relief by rolling on his side to face the wall, his head back on the pillow before he raised it again.

I do hear something. But what? He looked around. Lord, I know I'm free but just where am I? He jumped slightly as he felt a hand touch his face and then heard a voice muttering to him, that was the only way that he could describe it.

"Breck? Are you awake? Breck?" Neasa knelt by the bed, her hand on Breck's face, the other hand on his hair. "Breck? Please?"

"Where am I?" He had to clear his throat before he could speak.

"He said he was Doc. I had to come with you, Breck. It's my fault that you were hurt."

"It was?" Breck groaned as he rolled to his back and then pushed himself up on the pillows Neasa stacked behind him.

"It was. You tried to keep them from hurting me and they beat you up." Neasa felt the anger growing in her. "I don't know who they were or why they did this."

"We'll figure it out." Breck reached out a tentative hand to finger a lock of her hair. "You have beautiful hair."

Neasa frowned at him for a moment. "Breck?"

Breck sighed and then looked at her. "Are you sure that you're okay?"

"I am." Neasa settled on the floor beside the bed, one arm on it to prop up her head. "I couldn't leave you when they brought you in."

"You couldn't? Who?"

"Brought you in? Some friends of yours, Doc said. And one of their fathers."

"Barnabas and his father, Bruce. Was there a Brady?"

Neasa wrinkled her brow, in a very adorable manner Breck privately thought, before she nodded. "There was. He's a paramedic?"

"That he is. Listen, what time is it?"

"The time? Around four or five. Why?"

"Because I need up and I need my coffee."

Neasa just stared at him. "You need your coffee?"

"I do, Neasa. Now, if you'll excuse me, I need that bathrobe there at the end of the bed." He took it as Neasa handed it to him and then watched as he shifted to sit on the side of the bed. "It's okay, Neasa. I'll be okay. How be you go find the coffee? Do you drink that?"

"No, I don't. I like my hot chocolate but I doubt that I can find any."

Breck laughed softly. "Go and check out the tall cupboard by the fridge. I think you'll find some there. Even some mint-flavoured chocolate if I know Anna."

He was right, Neasa thought to herself, standing staring at the cupboard before she pulled out mint-flavoured hot chocolate. I need this. She had already started the coffee, Anna telling her the night before just to make herself at home.

Breck paused in the hallway, watching Neasa as she worked away in the dim light that she had put on. Lord, there is something about this lady that draws me to her. She is in difficulty and I don't know why. And I don't think it's all related to that find at the shelter. There is more going on. He walked quietly into the kitchen, startling Neasa as she turned.

"You're quiet."

"I know. I guess it's living on my own that has done that. Although Mom has always told me that I walked like a cat."

Neasa began to giggle, bringing a grin to his face. "A cat? What mother tells her son that?"

"Mine. She's just pointing out that cats walk quietly too."

"They can. Or they can be very loud." Neasa sat at the table, her mug in front of her, watching at Breck poured his coffee and then sat. "Nothing in it?"

"Sometimes I like it this way. This morning, I need a shot of just plain caffeine."

"I don't think that will work." Neasa grew quiet, lost in her thoughts, not seeing Breck rise again, and make toast for them. She just reached for a piece of what he set in front of her and began to eat it. "Breck? Do you know why it happened?"

Breck shook his head. "No, and that puzzles me. They seemed to be waiting for someone that first day."

"I think they were and that person never showed. I don't understand why they moved us."

"To keep us hidden." Breck reached for her hand, his thumb rubbing along it. "Did they hurt you?"

"No, just put that shackle on me. Didn't we talk about that?"

"I'm sorry, I can't remember. I do remember trying to protect you at the first house."

"You did. They beat you for that, Breck. I thought that they would kill you."

Breck nodded, his hand tightening on hers, a sense of foreboding coming over him. "May I pray with you? I think we are going to need it."

Neasa shrugged. "I guess. Breck?"

He shook his head at the unspoken question in her voice. "We'll pray, Neasa. Then we'll talk."

Doc hesitated in the doorway as he listened to Breck pray. *He has a powerful way of talking to You, Lord, now doesn't he?* He turned and walked away, his own prayers spoken in his heart.

Chapter 7

Neasa wandered Doc's living room, studying the artwork on the walls, the Scripture verses on the photos, and then the knickknacks. She was restless, she knew, and not just from the last few days. Something had happened over the past few months, something that she had not spoken to anyone about. Threats had been made against her, threats that she didn't understand. Neasa finally reached for the blanket on the back of the couch and plopped down into a corner of the couch, the blanket covering her. She was suddenly chilled, and that from fright

Breck had watched her from where he stood in the doorway speaking with Dallas, a police officer friend who had shown up. He moved towards Neasa, sitting beside her, finding her shifting to lean against him, his hand reaching for hers.

"Dallas? You wanted to speak with us? We have given our statements." Breck frowned. "At least, I think we did." He turned to stare at Neasa as she giggled. "What?"

"We did, Breck, but I know you don't remember doing that. Not that you had much of a one to give."

"Is that right?" His hand tightened on hers. "And how would you know that?"

"Because you gave it in the Emergency Department and you wouldn't let go of me." She grinned at him. "Not that I was leaving anyway."

"You weren't?" Breck watched her intently, reading something on her face that gave him hope that just maybe he had found a lady who would be willing to date him.

Dallas simply shook his head. "Come back to the present, you two. I need to ask you some questions."

"Ask away. We may or may not answer." Breck's gaze never left Neasa.

Staring at his friend, Dallas was not sure of what was going on. This was not Breck, he thought. Lord? Can You help, just a little? I need to talk to him and it doesn't look as if it's going to happen. "Breck? Please?"

"What is it you want to know?" Breck finally looked at Dallas.

"I need you to walk back through what happened. You have told the officers, but I would like to hear it again, from you two. Sometimes there is something that you don't remember when you give your statements. You know that from the other twelve."

"Twelve?" Neasa's free hand was waving in the air. "What are you two talking about?"

"The twelve men who live here. You've met them?" Breck watched her closely as he spoke

"I think so. And their wives." She stared between the two for them. "Wait a minute. You told me that some of your friends had had adventures and that I shouldn't be wanting one. That night when we escaped the hospital, you said that."

"That's right." Breck grinned at her again. "I did say that. All twelve of the men who live here, other than for Barnabas and myself, have had adventures, life-threatening in many cases, but through that, they found their lady loves."

"They did? I thought that only happened in books or movies or on television." Neasa stared at him, not sure if it was really what had happened.

"No, it happens in real life, Neasa." Breck looked past Dallas, not focusing on anything in particular. "It happens, Neasa." He finally turned to Dallas. "Where do you want us to start?"

"I think he wants us to start at the beginning." Neasa smirked at Breck as he looked at her. "Isn't that what they usually say?"

Dallas grinned, even as he shook his head. "You're right, Neasa. Now, which one of you goes first?"

"He can. He has less to say than I do." Neasa settled down tighter to Breck, finding comfort from just being near him, her eyes on their joined hands.

"I guess then, Dallas, I go first." Breck shut his eyes, trying to envision what had actually happened.

"I remember us leaving on your bike, Neasa, from the hospital. We didn't get very far before we realized that we were being followed. Neasa tried to evade them, but it didn't seem to work. At one point, we were able to switch places. She actually let me operate her motorbike." Breck looked down at her. "We headed for the downtown area, and I was able to back into an alleyway, with the lights off, watching as the two vehicles passed by. I thought that we had fooled them. I took off again, heading for Dan's when I was boxed in. I didn't have any choice but to stop. We were forced into a vehicle that took off at high speed. One of the men stayed with Neasa's bike.

"We were taken to a house just outside town. The old Millar place, Dallas. We were kept there for a day or so, I think. They tried to forced Neasa to sign some kind of paperwork and she refused. I stepped in when it looked as if they would start with an assault against her. I don't remember much after that.

"It did seem as if they were waiting for someone else to arrive. Only that person never did. They keep referring to the boss."

"The boss? Male or female?" Dallas looked up from his notes.

"I'm not sure. They didn't say much other than calling whoever it was that they were waiting for the boss." Breck sighed. "I can't even give a proper description of them, Dallas. They had on bulky jackets and hoodies with the hoods up and bandanas or masks of some kind across their lower faces."

Chapter 8

Dallas turned to Neasa, to find her watching him intently. Breck, you have yourself a very serious lady here, underneath all her fun. Something is going on with her, and I somehow think that you have just gotten involved over your head. Lord, protect my friend.

"Neasa? What is your story?"

"My story? I have no idea. All I did was unbury those bones." She sighed, leaning harder against Breck without realizing that she was and she felt his hand tighten on hers. "Okay. So, after they had beaten Breck and knocked him out. Or did they?" She looked up at Breck. "I think you fell, Breck, and hit your head on the edge of the table. You didn't move after that." She looked over at Dallas. "They moved us the next day to the old church. That's when they put the shackle on my wrist. They made sure that I couldn't reach Breck, even though I begged them to let me. They just laughed. There were three of them that day, four the day before. It's strange that they didn't take our phones. Mine had no charge left, but Breck roused enough to pull his out. He muttered something about sending a text message, but I'm not sure that he did."

"He sent a photo of some kind, Neasa. That allowed Barnabas and his father to recognize the building and find you two. Were they back at all after they left you there?"

"No. They left us there one day and then never came back. Breck's friends showed up the next day. I don't get it. Why us?" Neasa looked up at Breck, finding him watching her intently. "Breck?"

Breck shook his head. "I'm not sure, Neasa. I'm not sure that it is all related to those bones. It just doesn't make sense that it would be." He shared a look with Dallas. "Is there anything in your past that would have someone after you?"

"Me?" Neasa shrugged before she sighed. "Did Dad tell you that I was away for the last six months or so, working on my grandfather's farm?" When Breck nodded, she sighed again. "I was getting threats by letter, on my phone. I don't know who was doing that. It doesn't make sense. I haven't seen anything I should have. I behave myself. I don't associate with criminals or wannabe criminals or the shady side of life in town." She became quiet. "Nor does Nevin. This started about a month after I got there."

"Did you keep everything?" Dallas hoped that she had.

"I did. I have it all in a safety deposit box. They were text messages, so I was able to save them that way." She reached into her pocket. "You'll want my phone. I have another one that I can use. With a different number."

"That's good. Who all has that number?" Dallas looked up as she remained quiet. "Neasa? Who all has your new phone number?"

—

39

"No one at present. I just got the phone the day before we found the bones. I was planning on letting my family know and just a couple of friends."

"Good. Let me have the number. Breck will want it. I would suggest that the fellows here have it as well."

"Really?" Neasa looked mutinous for a moment.

"It's for your own safety, Neasa." Breck spoke up. "If for some reason you need me and I can't make it, you can call any one of the fellows or their ladies for that matter, and they will come and help you."

Neasa finally nodded before she whispered. "Okay. But it's at home. If someone is after me, how do I go there? I would only bring trouble to Dad and Nevin and then Mom when she comes home."

Breck blew out a breath, his eyes on Dallas. "I will take you, Neasa. And there is an apartment here in the building that you can use. Right beside me."

"There is?" Neasa looked up at him. "That would be okay? I mean, I don't want to bring any trouble here." She frowned as the two men began to laugh. "What did I say that was so funny?"

Breck wrapped his arm around her, their hands still joined, and hugged her. "It's okay, Neasa. It's just that there has been trouble brought to the building before. Twelve times in fact."

"Your twelve friends, right? What else should I know before I move in here? And I'm not saying that I am." Neasa stared up at Breck as he tried hard to smother his grin. "And wipe that smirk off your face, buster."

Dallas began to laugh even harder. "Breck, your lady is a spitfire. You have your hands full."

Neasa glared at Dallas. "Whose lady? And when was I to be informed of that fact?"

Chapter 9

Neasa looked around her childhood bedroom, wiping a tear from her face. She was moving out and moving on, she thought. She had had an apartment away from here, she thought, before she had moved home the previous year, but this was different. She just hadn't settled into one since then and being away at her grandparents' meant that she hadn't needed one. Neasa drew the zipper closed on her bag and then looked around once more, just ensuring that she had what she really needed. She knew that she could come back and forth but this was the move that she needed to make.

Breck stood in the hallway watching her, before he walked towards her, just reaching to draw her into a hug, feeling her hug him back. His voice whispered a prayer in her ear. Neasa was sure that she felt him kiss the top of her head when he finished but decided that she was imagining things.

"Ready?" Breck's voice was quiet before he reached for the duffel bags on her bed.

"I think so. I hate doing this when Dad's at work. But I'm not sure if I should be around him."

"We can stop by the job site. Does he expect you to be working?" Breck was concerned about her doing just that.

"He hasn't said. I should though, but it's almost the end of the season for us. The job at the shelter was the last one." Neasa searched Breck's face, seeing nothing but caring and compassion on it. "Breck? I'm not sure what to do now. He usually doesn't do much over the winter, just plans for the next year."

"Are you going to be working for him next year?" Breck shut the back door of his truck, and then stood, leaning against it, watching her.

Neasa shrugged. "I doubt it. I wanted to get back to what I had trained as, but I'm not sure now that I even want to do that." She sighed, a woebegone look on her face.

"And what had you trained in?"

"I had trained as a chef and had been working in a really nice restaurant, but it just got to be too much. I didn't like the big city living."

"Then, take the time you need to decide. Volunteer if you want to. I know Cadee's parents would be glad if you did. They prepare meals for the shelter residents." Breck held up a hand. "I'm not saying that's what you should do. Just think about what you want to do." He helped her into the truck and then stood, staring around. Someone is out there, I can feel them watching us. Lord, protect my lady. He was not aware of how he had just prayed, he was that concerned about Neasa.

Neasa watched as Breck pulled back onto the Barnabas Foundation grounds and into his designated spot before he turned off his truck and just sat.

"Breck?" Neasa finally spoke, not sure what was going on with him.

—

"Neasa? This worried me, what you said about someone sending you those messages. You never said anything to anyone?" He looked over at her.

"No, I really didn't believe it at first, and then it was so busy on the farm that I just sort of ignored them. I guess I shouldn't have, but it really didn't register with me that it was dangerous." She stared out the side window, biting at her lip. "What do I do, Breck? How do I stay safe?"

"That we can work on. Dallas will be around again, I'm sure of that. He'll need to talk with you about the messages and what they have found out. But that could take a while."

"I know. It's not a high priority. It's not life and death for me, at least not yet."

"No, it's not, but you are a lady being threatened. That doesn't happen."

"But no one can stop it, can they?" She finally reached to open the door, not waiting for him to come around.

Breck sighed to himself before he levered himself out of the truck, a groan coming from him. He was still very sore, after his adventures, he thought. He reached into the back for her bags, letting her take her laptop case.

"This way." Breck opened the lobby door and then watched as she stood, fascinated with the openness and the two sitting areas opposite one another.

"This is nice. Fireplaces as well. And the stained glass up there? I like that."

"Barnabas' mother had some of these ideas. We can spend time down here as friends, now that the guys are married. It helps." He pointed to the stairs. "We can walk up or we can take the elevator."

"Walk, I think. I need to do that." Neasa stopped, her eyes on him. "But are you okay to do that?"

"I'm fine, Neasa." Breck paused in front of a door, pulling out a set of keys. "This is the one for you to use. There is no charge, Neasa."

"What? That can't be right!"

"It is, Neasa. The Foundation keeps apartments here for use, such as for you. Some of the other ladies have used them as well. It's part of their mandate of encouraging others." He unlocked the door, opened it, and then waited patiently for Neasa to walk in.

Neasa entered, not quite sure what she was walking in to, a soft sound coming from her as she saw the beautiful, comforting decor and colours. "This is beautiful, Breck. So warm and welcoming." She finally made her way back to the hallway, where he still stood. "My stuff?"

Breck grinned. "Your stuff, is it? I'll drop it into the master bedroom. I think some of the ladies shopped for you, but if you need anything, let me know." He paused. "What about a vehicle?"

"Just find my motorbike." She sighed. "I need to talk to the insurance company about it, but I'm not sure how to explain it."

—

45

"I can help you with that." Breck sighed as he felt his phone vibrate. "Excuse me for a moment." He peered at the text message. "It's Dallas. They have found your motorbike. It's okay. He says they'll take it to the police garage, go over it and then release it to you."

"Oh, thank goodness. I saved up for that. It was my first real purchase." Neasa paused, her eyes on him. "Breck? Thank you."

Breck shrugged. "It's what I do, Neasa. It's who I am. And besides, you're special." He grinned at her and then shut the door behind him, not seeing the look that softened her face.

Chapter 10

With just a low light on, Neasa curled up on the couch, her inevitable cup of hot chocolate in her hand, and studied the living room. This is a nice place. I can't get too comfortable, though, as I will have to leave. Eventually. She set her cup on the end table and then laid her head on her outstretched arm, her face turning dreamy as she thought of Breck. He is such a compassionate, caring man. I wonder that he has never married, but right now, he's the friend that I need. Neasa reached for her phone, pulling up her text messages, finding one from Breck. She smiled as she read it, and then responded to it, telling him good night.

Breck reached for his own phone, smiling as he read Neasa's text message. She's a sweet lady, Lord. I wonder that she's never married. I don't want to hurt her, and I am afraid that I might do just that. He stopped as he read the one from Dallas and shook his head. I'll call in the morning, he thought. Tonight, I just need to sleep. He set his phone aside, turned out his light, and then spent the next while in prayer, Neasa one of the ones that he petitioned hardest for.

The next morning, Breck stared down at his desk, studying the paperwork that needed to be done. Neasa, I'm sorry. I need to do this but I will catch up with you, by lunch. I promise. He sent off a quick text to her and then immersed himself into the paperwork, looking up as his door opened.

"Brody? How are you?"

"I'm fine, but how are you?" Brody sat in one of the chairs in front of the desk.

Breck shrugged. "As okay as I can be. We were to meet the other morning."

"We were, but that's okay. I just dropped in to see how you were and ask what we can do for you."

"Right now?" Breck just grinned. "I can't think of anything but if I do, I'll certainly ask." He paused. "Neasa is in the apartment next to mine. We all felt it best that she not be at her parents' for now. Maybe some of the ladies could stop by?"

Brody grinned. "Ker is already planning that. She and Imly and Jaxcy, I think. A welcome to the building visit. Neasa won't be leaving."

"She won't?" Breck stared at his friend, his eyes narrowing at the look on Brody's face. "Not happening, Brody."

"I say otherwise. I've seen her around the church. She's your lady, Breck. She's the one that you need to complete you. But on another note, Ker has asked what the building does for holidays, if there's anything in particular that we do, decorations, etc."

"You know, we never really have, not outside our own apartments. She's wanting to decorate?"

Brody nodded. "All the ladies are. They think we need something in the lobby, just to brighten it as we come in and out. I told her that I'd ask."

Breck sat back, his eyes on his friend. "I can't see that it would hurt. Tell them to go ahead, be modest with what they do, and then bring me the bills. I'll okay it with the board, but I don't see a problem, given that it is our home."

Brody stood. "That's what we thought you'd say. You're in our prayers, Breck. This time, we get to help you. Call us." He walked away, the door closing quietly behind him.

Breck rose, staring at his desk, and then cleared away paperwork before he reached for his schedule. Nothing more today, he thought. I need to find Neasa, glancing at his watch. I'm sure that she's found something to do but I need to make sure. He headed for the stairs, his steps slowing as he reached the lobby, his eyes on Neasa as she sat on one of the couches in the seating area. There were two but she had chosen the one nearest his office. He smiled, wondering if she had done that on purpose.

Sitting beside her, Breck waited. When he spoke, Neasa jumped and turned to stare at him, her face white, fear making her eyes huge.

"Breck? When did you get here?"

"Just now. You were lost in thought." He reaching for her hand, finding it cold. "You're chilled."

"No, not really. I am just trying to make sense of all this." Neasa sighed. "Can you?"

"Not at present. We don't have enough information. Has Dallas been in touch about your bike?"

"No, not yet. When I talked to him last, he said it would be a couple of days. That's what I need. To go for a really long ride. It always helps to clear my mind."

"I don't have a bike, but I have a truck. We could go for a really long drive. Grab some lunch and have a picnic." He grinned as she stared at him.

"A picnic? At this time of year? Breck!" Then she frowned. "Did you just ask me out?"

Breck thought for a moment. "Yeah, I guess I did. Would you do me the honour of going for a nice long ride and then having a picnic with me?"

Neasa tilted her head before she nodded. "Thank you, Breck. I think that is exactly what I need to do." She waited for him to stand. "Well? Didn't you say something about lunch?"

Breck laughed as he pulled her to her feet and then through the door to his truck, tucking her inside. When he had seated himself, he turned, laughter still on his face. "I did. Thank you, Neasa. You're a beautiful lady with a kind heart."

Chapter 11

Late that afternoon, Barnabas stood and watched as Breck and Neasa walked back towards him, hand in hand before he shook his head. Brady had been right, he thought. There is interest there. Brady had been adamant that morning that Breck had found his lady. Barnabas had replied that he didn't think he had.

Breck looked up, surprise on his face for a moment. "Barnabas, you're waiting for us?"

"I am. Dallas was around. He needed to speak with both of you. He said that he'd be back early this evening." He turned to Neasa. "Neasa, my parents are around. They would like it if you would come for dinner tonight."

"They would? I really need to talk with my Dad." Neasa was hesitant.

"He's invited as is Nevin. Mom talked to your mother earlier." He grinned at Neasa groaned. "That was bad?"

"Knowing Mom? It might be. She might have let out a secret or two."

Breck grinned, mischief on his face. "You have secrets? You didn't tell me that."

She shoved at him with her shoulder, finding that she was more and more comfortable around him. "I have secrets. Barnabas, he's your old friend. Does he have any secrets that I should know about?"

Barnabas began to laugh, despite Breck's protest that he had no secrets, causing the men and ladies in the lobby to glance their way. "Oh, I think he does. One or two."

"Only one or two? That's not too many for me to discover." She tugged at her hand. "If I'm to go out for dinner, I need to go get ready. Dressy or casual?"

"Casual, Neasa. We don't dress up any more than we have to."

She stared at Barnabas. "That's not what I expected. Considering you're on the board here as is your father, I thought that you'd be in suits and ties all the time."

Breck shook his head at Barnabas. "I know from what you said that is how the boards you have dealt with have been. Not this one. We are more interested in the person than the dress. It's part of how we try to encourage others." Breck watched her face closely as she thought through his words.

Neasa finally shook her head, a grin on her face. "I'll figure it out. I always do. Breck, if you're invited for the meal, come find me." She ran quickly for the stairs and then disappeared from sight.

Breck watched her leave before he glanced around the lobby. "I see we have an audience."

Barnabas laughed, thinking that was funny. "You do, Breck. It's your turn for the spotlight. And we're all happy for you." He pointed towards the corridor to the offices. "Do you have some time?"

"I do. I should be checking on my messages." Breck was hesitant to do just that.

"Leave it for now, my friend. Let's go pray for you and your lady. I fear for you two."

Breck nodded, watching Barnabas closely. "Thanks, Barnabas. She's running from something or someone. I'm just not sure what or who."

"They all were, Breck. Every one of the ladies was. That's where our fellows stepped in."

Breck nodded, slipping down into the chair he favoured in the office. "Barnabas? There's more than what you said."

"There is, Breck. Dallas will be back out. He asked that you be available, both you and Neasa. He was almost angry if I could describe how he was."

"At us?"

"No, at whatever is going on." Barnabas leaned forward, his arms on the desk. "How can I pray for you, Breck?"

Breck shrugged. "I'm usually the one asking that, aren't I? I really don't know, to tell you the truth. I'm in uncharted waters here."

"I know that. Dad and I were talking. Neasa is going to need something to fill her time. I spoke with Dan after the board met. We're putting the work at the shelter on hold until the spring. We felt it best, given that the police may need back into the site. He said that he doesn't have anything on the books, as he put it, for now, not until spring. He's worried about her."

———

53

"I know he is. I'll see what I can find for her to do. She's a trained chef, but I got the impression that she's reluctant to take that back up."

"She is? You know, the board was looking at setting up to do meal deliveries for the seniors and shut-ins. Would she be interested in heading that up?"

Breck shrugged. "I have no idea. Let your Dad talk to her. He might get a better sense than either one of us." Breck yawned. "I'm sorry. I'm beat."

"I know. Take off, Breck. It's Friday. Come back on Monday to start over." Barnabas watched his friend walk away, a prayer in his heart for him and his lady.

Chapter 12

Breck watched Neasa closely that evening, seeing how exhausted that she was. He finally reached for a small pillow, dropping it against his leg, and then leaned over to whisper to her.

"You can lay down, Neasa. They won't mind." He nodded as she looked up at him and then with a grateful sigh, did that, her head on the pillow, her legs curled up on the couch.

Elizabeth had been watching and reached for a blanket to cover her. "She's tired, Breck." Her hand rested on Breck's head.

"She is, Elizabeth. And from more than just the last few days. We have a chance to talk today, but I won't break her confidence." His arm rested around Neasa.

"Nor would we ask you to." Elizabeth exchanged a glance with Bruce. "What can we do for her?"

Dan had watched his daughter closely, seeing how she was turning to Breck, and not himself or Nevin. "Right now, Elizabeth? Just let it lie. She likes to mull things over. If she wants help, she'll ask for it."

Nevin, Barnabas, and Beck exchanged glances, knowing that Dan was reading his daughter wrong. Nevin sighed. Even he could not get Neasa to open up to him. That had never happened in the past. They were close, this brother and sister, sharing their thoughts and wishes and dreams with one another.

Dallas stood for a moment, watching the group, Bruce standing beside him.

"She's sleeping?"

"She is, Dallas. She's exhausted." Bruce watched Breck closely, thinking of him as another son. "Breck thinks that is more than just the last few days. He talked with me, told me I could tell you that."

"I'm sure that it is. She's running, Bruce."

"I know she is. I see all the signs. And she's run to Breck, not her family. I think that has surprised her father."

Dallas glanced at Dan, finding him in conversation with Barnabas. "It will be hard for him to let go, you know? I had a long talk with Will today."

"He and Dan have been friends for many years. They grew up together, just as I did with them." Bruce shook his head. "But until something happens, or she speaks freely, we can't do much."

"No, unfortunately, we can't." Dallas sighed as his phone chimed and he excused himself to answer it. When he returned, it was to simply excuse himself from the gathering. He had a crime scene to get to.

Late that evening, only Breck and Neasa were left with Barnabas, the others heading home. Barnabas handed Breck a new mug of coffee before he sat in his favourite chair, a sigh coming from him.

<hr>

"You need a vacation, Barnabas." Breck watched him closely. "All this with the men have worn you out."

"It has, Breck." Barnabas sighed again, his eyes closing for a moment. "And you as well."

"Well, yeah, there's that too." Breck's hand tightened on Neasa's. Over the course of the evening, her hand had found his.

"Dan seemed surprised that Neasa wasn't turning to him or Nevin."

"We talked about that. She wants a different perspective on what she's going through. Her family is too close to her." Breck pulled his upper lip down over his teeth, a habit he had when he was uncertain about something. "I need to talk with you and the fellows, but I need to talk to Neasa first."

"About what?" Neasa sat up, sleepily pushing the hair back from her eyes. "What I'm going through? How could they help?"

"They have helped solve all the adventures, as we call them, that they each had. They all have different ideas and thoughts, work through them, and then pool them." Breck studied her, seeing the shadows in her eyes. "I won't talk to them if you say no, Neasa. I won't break your confidence."

"I know you won't." She turned to Barnabas. "How do I do it though? It's just random thoughts, ideas, impressions. Nothing really solid."

—

"I would say that we all meet, the ladies as well if you want. They've helped as well. We don't discount them just because they're ladies."

"That's refreshing." Neasa leaned against Breck. "I need to go home, Breck. It's late."

"I know it is. Here, up you go." Breck stood, reaching for Neasa's hand.

Neasa whispered a soft thank you to Barnabas before she walked away, tugging Breck with her. Barnabas watched as they left, a prayer for his friend and his lady rising.

Chapter 13

The next afternoon, Neasa wandered the conference room that had been set up with computers, whiteboards, printers, faxes, and whatever supplies were needed. She was impressed, to put it mildly, and told Breck that. He had grinned at her comment before he turned to answer a question from Branigan.

Berneen, Baird's wife, approached Neasa, not sure how to do just that.

"Neasa? Have you everything that you need?"

Neasa turned. "It's Berneen, right? Thank you. I do. I understand that I have you ladies to thank for that."

Berneen shrugged. "It's what we do, Neasa. It's part of being in the Foundation family. We are encouraged to be encouragers."

"That's a mouthful." Neasa grinned. "I understand that it was named after Barnabas and also the Barnabas in the Bible. I have always loved how he was such an encourager to Paul and to the churches."

"Me, too." Berneen directed their steps to the small kitchen area. "They set this up to provide coffee, tea, water, juice. The cupboards hold snacks. We make sure the fridge has fresh fruit and veggies."

"You seem to think of everything." Neasa accepted the cup of hot chocolate handed to her by

Jaxcy. "Thank you. Someone must have squealed on me."

"He did. He was adamant that we keep hot chocolate, mint flavoured preferred, here now. He's taking care of you, Neasa."

"He is." Neasa's face softened as her eyes sought out Breck. "He is. He's a good listener."

"He is. Hagen's twin sisters, Hailey and Hollie, think of him as their big brother. He has helped them a lot with different things."

"He would. He's that kind of man. He also has a wonderful way of praying."

"He does, Neasa. I can't tell you how many times one of his prayers have lifted me up when I needed it." Berneen turned to face the other woman. "We'll need to tell you all our stories. I understand Breck told you that you didn't need one of our adventures."

Neasa began to laugh. "He did. I told him that I wanted one. But now that I seem to be involved in one? I think he was right. Just don't tell him that."

"Not tell who what?" Breck grinned at Neasa as he came to stand beside her.

"I'm not telling and neither are these ladies." Neasa shook her finger at him even as she grinned. "So, tell me. What have you discovered so far?"

Breck stared at her, even as the ladies began to laugh.

——

"She's got you there, Breck." Berneen reached to hug Neasa, surprising her. "It's not often we get one up on Breck. You just did. You're good for him."

Neasa stared at Breck for a moment before she nodded. "You know? I think you're right. Someone has to keep him in line." That brought more gales of laughter from the ladies with Breck protesting that he didn't need to be kept in line.

Barnabas turned from where he stood at the front of the room, in conversation with Buckley and Brandon, and shook his head.

"He's met his match. She'll be good for him." Buckley grinned.

"I agree." Brandon watched the couple closely, seeing how close Neasa had moved to Breck. "What's going on with her?"

"That we don't know yet. Breck just mentioned to me that she had moved back from a big city, not liking that life, but that he felt there was more to it than that. She's passed her phone over to Dallas."

"Phone? Messages?" Brandon looked at Barnabas for confirmation.

"I would say so. Neither one is saying."

"That incident at the shelter? Any word on it?" Buckley sipped at his coffee before he set the mug down on a table.

"No. Dallas didn't think there would be. He's not the one investigating it right now. Not unless his supervisor pulls him in. It will take time, he said." Barnabas was frustrated with that. "The board has decided to wait until spring to move forward with that once more." He turned as Bradon approached. "Bradon?"

"Dallas just had this dropped off for you. The officer asked that you get it right away." He handed over an envelope.

"Thanks, Bradon. Buckley, let's get our meeting started. I see all the ladies are here."

"They are. Hey, everyone, let's find our seats and spend time in prayer, just like always." Buckley watched as the men and ladies sorted themselves out into twos before he walked towards Bruce. "Bruce?"

"Sure, Buckley. Let's find our chairs. I feel that we need this prayer time today. And I have no idea why."

Chapter 14

Neasa looked around later that afternoon, wandering the apartment that she was living in. She was tired, she thought, of having her life on hold. That was how it had felt. She missed her bike as well, normally heading out on long rides when she felt like this. Maybe a run, she thought? Dressing quickly, she headed for the stairs, finding Jaxcy heading up.

"Neasa? Just who I was looking for." Jaxcy turned to walk back down with her. "Oh! You're dressed for a run. Have you seen the gym?"

Neasa's head shot around. "There's a gym? Breck didn't tell me that."

Jaxcy grinned. "He didn't? And yes, there is. This way. Hagen has a woodworking shop attached to the back. She crafts toys and puzzles. Most of her work is sold online."

"I need to look at that. But first, the gym." Neasa stared around the gym. "This is nice. Much better than some of the gyms I've been to over the years."

"Barnabas makes sure to have all the equipment kept up to date. It's part of what he docs. The Foundation looks after us."

"I can see that." Neasa moved towards a treadmill. "This is a nice one. I keep repeating that word. I need to find a new one."

Jaxcy broke out into laughter at that. "And there are trails around here that are great for walking, even taking you to the lake. But I wouldn't advise that right now." She stepped onto an adjacent treadmill and made the adjustments that she wanted.

"And why not?" Neasa was puzzled.

"Because of what you're going through. It's not likely safe. The bad guys, as Hollie refers to them, have actually come right into our building."

Neasa nodded, knowing that was the case. She sighed to herself even as she began to run. How do I do this, Lord? I feel that I am bringing a lot of danger to these ladies and the little ones. How can I solve this and then move on, without harm coming to anyone?

Jaxcy watched closely as Neasa abruptly stepped away from the machine and then left, her heart rising in prayer for her new friend.

Neasa stood outside the gym, staring around before she moved towards what she thought were gardens. Her eyes widened in surprise as she saw the fruit trees and bushes. This is so wonderful, she thought. She turned as she heard footsteps. Burnie stood there, watching, a closed look on his face before he smiled.

"Neasa? I'm Burnie. I think that we've met."

"I think so." Neasa walked towards him. "You're an author."

"I am." He turned to walk beside her as she headed for the rose garden. "This garden here? All the ladies love it. The roses bloom for months."

———

"They do? I would like to see it but I'll be long gone before they bloom in the spring." Neasa sank down onto a bench, her eyes on the ground. "Burnie? You had an adventure?"

"I did. It was quite the one as well. But I met my beautiful Muir and rescued her as well as her Granny."

"Granny? Oh, I know her. She makes sure that she speaks to me every time I'm at the church. She's so sweet."

"She is. She raised Muir from a baby after Muir's parents were killed in a plane crash. Long story. We'll have you over for dinner one night and tell you all about it."

"You will? I see. Making plans for me?" Mischief sparkled in her eyes as she watched him.

Burnie spluttered with his words for a moment before he too began to laugh. "Does Breck know what a treasure he has?"

"A treasure? And who has? As far as I know, we're not a couple. And not likely to be." Neasa shook her head at that.

"I think otherwise, Neasa, but it's up to Breck to tell you."

"Burnie, can I ask something else? I don't want to seem insensitive or impudent, but I notice that all of you have the same initials."

"We do. God laid it on Barnabas' heart that he needed to find men to bring here to work. All had to have the same initials as he does. All would be orphans. We come from every province and territory

—

in Canada, except for Breck and Barnabas who are from this area. The Foundation pays our wages, letting our employers find others as they need to without financial hardship. We all volunteer at something as well. And our wives are paid wages from the Foundation as well. This is all part of their mandate of being encouragers.”

“Wow! I didn’t realize that. It’s not noised around, is it?”

“No. It’s not. I mean we could talk about it if we wanted to, but we don’t.”

“I see.” Neasa grew quiet before she looked up at him once more. “Your ladies? I see that their last names are all starting with the letter “D” and that their names go in alphabetical order. But there is no one that starts with “A”.”

“No, there isn’t. We all think that will be Barnabas’ lady. Only we have no idea who she is or where she is.” Burnie stretched out his legs, his hands going into his jeans’ pockets.

“You do?” Neasa nodded. “Of course, she would be. I just find it interesting how it has worked out. He looks sad sometimes when he doesn’t think anyone is watching him.”

“He does. It’s becoming more frequent. Muir and I think that he had a lady who walked out on him. We also think that he’ll take off and try and find her at some point, just to close that chapter.”

"That's so sad." Neasa grew thoughtful before she was on her feet. "I need to keep moving, Burnie. I'm sorry. I'm restless."

"And you will be, until whatever it is that is weighing you down disappears. Talk to any one of us, please? Breck has always been there for us, no matter what. We want to do the same for him and for you. He's chosen you, Neasa, whether you realize it or not."

Chapter 15

Breck stared at Dallas as he spoke before he reached for the picture. He stared down at it. This was taken yesterday, he thought, as he and Neasa had walked around the building.

"Where did you get this?"

"It was dropped off at the front desk. We're pulling the security feed to see if we can make out who it was. The desk officer had turned away for a moment and when she turned back, it was there."

"That's from yesterday. They're watching her closely."

"Or you." Dallas nodded as Breck's eyes shot up once more to stare at him. "You, Breck. I know that you don't have any dark secrets. At least, I think that you don't. But you're involved with Neasa. Someone is after her and they're going to go after you."

"I know, Dallas. Neasa and I have talked. She's been open with me. Unfortunately, I can't share what she has told me, without asking her for permission. We're taking all the precautions that we can, but it seems as if they're not enough."

"They're never enough." Dallas was frustrated, turning as a tap came to the door and it opened.

"Breck? I can come back." Neasa's voice was very quiet and withdrawn.

Breck was to her side, drawing her into his office before she had a chance to leave. "No, it's okay, darling. We need to talk with you anyway."

"About what?" Her eyes saw the photo that Breck had dropped on his desk. "That's us."

"It is. Someone has been around, taking pictures of us. We're off on that adventure that you so wanted."

"I don't want it anymore. Not at all." She thrust the envelope that she had been holding at him. "This came today. How did they know that I was here?"

"Drop it on the desk, Neasa." Dallas watched her hesitate. "On the desk, Neasa." He pulled out a pair of latex gloves. "You've read it, but I need to preserve it as much as I can."

Neasa paled as she did just what he asked. "Dallas?"

"I need to talk to you about your phone messages, but first this." Dallas carefully slid the letter from the envelope and opened it, his face growing grim as he did so. "Neasa, what did you go and get mixed up in?"

"Nothing. Absolutely nothing. I went to work, went home, went to church, went to the gym. Went shopping. I kept to myself. I really had no friends there." She paled as she saw Dallas' face before she grew angry. "I have done nothing to warrant this."

"I know, Neasa. I know. I just need to ask the questions." He read the letter before his eyes raised to Breck and then back to Neasa. "Neasa? Where did you work?"

"At some fancy-dancy restaurant in the downtown area of the town. I lived nearby. I didn't have contact with any of the customers. The wait staff was always changing over, which I found strange. I had been there for about two years when I left." She bit at her lip. "I found that strange.'"

"It is strange. Let me have the name of the restaurant and the owner's name." He wrote them down before he looked back at the letter. "This is very specific about an event. Do you remember it?"

Neasa shook her head. "Not really. I know that there were sometimes private dinners. I never saw the guests. I only cooked." She poked at the letter with a slim index finger. "What did they think that I saw?"

"'That's what we have to determine." Dallas gathered the letter and envelope back up and sealed them into an evidence bag before tucking it back into a pocket. "Listen, you two. You need to take precautions. Breck, you are well aware of what needs to be done. Neasa? Do you have transportation other than your bike?"

Neasa shrugged. "I can get something. I need to, now that the weather's turning colder. Why?"

"Because you need to. You can't be out on your bike. It's too dangerous."

Neasa's temper flared at that. "Right now, I don't see any danger. Other than some text messages that make no sense, that letter that says I saw something that I didn't, and that picture, I see nothing to worry me." She was gone before either man could react.

Breck ran after her, finding her on her motorbike, pulling away. He stopped in frustration before he ran for his truck. Neasa, please? Let me talk with you. He followed her until she finally pulled over, just sitting waiting for him to approach her.

"Neasa?"

"Breck. Go home. I don't want you around me."

"That's not happening, Neasa. I will not walk away from you." Breck rested his hand on the handlebars of the motorbike.

"I don't want you hurt. Please? Go home?" Neasa finally looked up at him, her face haunted.

"What did you remember, Neasa?"

She shook for a moment before she nodded. "I did remember something. Take me home, Breck. I mean to Dad's. I need to leave my bike there."

Breck watched her as she pulled away before he was back into his truck and following her as closely as he could. He waited as she settled her bike into the garage and then ran for his truck, ducking inside and buckling up. Neasa prayed that her family had not seen her. She didn't know how she would explain her movements, of not coming in to see them, and just leaving with Breck.

—

Chapter 16

Breck pulled into a local coffee shop, running in and out quickly with an order for them, handing Neasa her hot chocolate, setting his coffee into the cup holder. He pulled away, searching for somewhere that they could talk, finally just deciding on the parking lot at the local library. Before Neasa could speak, he simply reached for her hand and prayed for her.

Neasa blinked as he finished. She couldn't think of another friend who would do that, just sit and pray with her. She felt his hand squeeze hers and she then clung to his. She needed that contact.

"What did you remember, Neasa?" Breck finally spoke, his voice quiet.

"I'm not sure what it was. I can remember one night one of the wait staff coming back into the kitchen, her face white. She was shaking. I couldn't get her to tell me what happened. She just took off her apron, found her purse, and walked out. Someone else had to pick up for her. They never said anything. I never saw her again, but there was a report of a murder. The description seemed like her, but I never heard a name. Could that be it?"

"It could be. They may think that she said something. We'll need to let Dallas know." Breck's thumb rubbed against her hand. "What else?"

"I can remember being followed one night as I was walking from the bus. I heard the footsteps that tapped after me, stopping every time that I did. I ran the final block and locked myself into my apartment. That was about a month before I came home. I put in my notice the next day and just walked away. I didn't have much in the apartment. It never felt like home."

"You came home and then went to work on your grandfather's farm." Breck stared out through the windshield. "How did that work out?"

She shrugged. "It got me away from the city and then away from here. I needed space to think. I'm not sure how much thinking I did. I worked until I dropped every night, even though Pops tried to make me not. I was driven, I guess, Breck."

"Driven to forget?" At her nod, he sighed. "Where do we go, Neasa? How do we protect you?"

Neasa stared out the side window before she spoke, her voice sounding tiny in the truck cab.

"I don't know, Breck. How do you protect against someone that you can't see, that you don't know?"

"We have done just that, Neasa. Twelve times. Sure, they were injured, some had to be brought back to life, but God protected us in so many ways. He will protect you. All I ask?" His voice died away, not sure what to say or even how to say it.

Neasa waited before she turned to him. "What do you ask?"

"I ask, Neasa, that you let me walk beside you through this. You are a beautiful, funny, adorable lady who loves my God so much. I would like to be that man who protects you, Neasa." He didn't look at her, not wanting to see her rejection of him.

Neasa had to swallow hard. "Breck?" When he didn't look at her, she tugged at his hand, causing him to look at her. "Do you mean that?" At his nod, she closed her eyes, a tear tracking down her cheek. "Thank you. I have waited all my life for those very words." She opened her eyes to find him watching her intently. "Will you?"

"I will. I don't want to see you hurt, Neasa, but there's more there. I would like to see where we go, if we go anywhere, in our relationship. I have never ever been attracted to someone. Not until you. People think it's strange. I have talked to both my parents. Mom just hugged me and told me that if God wanted me single, then I needed to accept that and live my life for Him. Dad hugged me as well, told me to wait for my Proverbs 31 lady."

"Proverbs 31 lady? I like that." Neasa stared out the side window again. "I'm just not sure that I'm a Proverbs 31 lady."

"You are to me, Neasa." Breck's voice was barely audible. "Now, what else can you tell me?"

Her head shot around as she stared at him before she began to laugh. "Only you, Breck, could tell me what you did, and then ask that?"

Breck was puzzled until he thought back over what he had said and then he too laughed.

—

"I'm sorry. I shouldn't have done that."

"I can see life is going to be interesting." She watched as he reached for his phone which had been vibrating for a while. "I wondered when you were going to answer that."

He shook his finger at her. "When I'm with you, you are my priority, the most important thing at the moment." He looked at his text messages. "Barnabas is looking for us. He needs to talk with us, as soon as we can make it. I don't like that. He doesn't do that unless there is an emergency."

"Anything else?" She reached into a pocket for her own phone. "Dad left a voice mail." She listened to it. "It's okay. He just wanted to make sure I was okay. He found my motorbike in the garage but not me. He'll have to get used to that."

"He will. I'll talk with him if you like. In fact, I need to, if we're to start dating."

"Start dating, is it? And talking to my Dad? That sounds serious, buster."

Chapter 17

Barnabas watched as Breck and Neasa walked towards him across the parking lot from where Breck had parked. The men of the building had gathered in the conference room, taking the information that he and Dallas had given them and begun their search. Not that they had a lot at the present time, he thought. We need to get Neasa to talk to us, and I'm not sure that we can.

"Barnabas? You called?" Breck grinned at his friend before he sobered. "You have something to talk to us about."

"I do. Dallas was around. The crime lab had a look at the threat and the picture. They found something in the letter." Barnabas turned to walk back towards the building. "The fellows are working on what they can."

"I figured that they would be. It's different this time."

Barnabas gave a quick grin. "It is. It's you that they're investigating. Not one of them, with you leading."

Neasa paused in her walk, her eyes on the gardens. "What do they do?"

"I'm not sure if I can explain it all. Each one has their own way of searching. It always seems to work."

Barnabas paused at the conference room door. "If you ask each one, Neasa, they will explain it to you."

She shrugged. "Not that it really matters. I was just curious."

"Ask them, Neasa. If you don't, I will and have them each talk to you. This is your life that we're speaking of. You need to know." Breck was firm with her, not letting her back down from her question.

"Boy, you're bossy." Neasa yanked open the door and entered, letting it close behind her.

Breck stared at it until he turned to Barnabas, to find his friend with a grin on his face. His eyes narrowed.

"You think this is funny?"

"In a way, I do, Breck. She's got your number. She's exactly what you need." Barnabas disappeared into the room, leaving Breck staring at the closed door.

Breck cautiously opened the door and peeked in, grinning to himself as he saw Neasa seated beside Baird, watching him as he worked away. He could tell that she was asking questions, just from how Baird was working.

Buckley stood beside the door, watching Breck.

"Are you coming in or not?"

"In. At least I think I am. Barnabas had information for me."

"He does. Here. This is your copy. Your lady has gotten herself involved in something pretty nasty."

"That's what Neasa and I have already decided." Breck glanced through it. "Here. This name? That's likely the wait staff that she says walked out. She thought that the lady had been killed."

"What kind of restaurant was it?" Buckley pulled out a chair and sat beside Breck.

"That I am not sure of. She says it was a high-end one, but the staff kept changing all the time. She was followed home one night and that's when she gave her notice and moved home."

"Only whoever it was followed her?"

"I would think so." Breck paused. "I wonder how she got her things here. She couldn't on her bike."

"I sent them by bus, Breck. It was the cheapest way. Not that there was much." Neasa stood beside him, her hand on his shoulder.

"Have you gone through the boxes?"

Neasa nodded. "I did. I unpacked everything and put the boxes out for recycling. There wasn't anything there that wasn't mine if that's what you are thinking."

"I am." Breck pointed to the chair beside him. "I saw you talking with Baird."

"I was. He was actually able to explain what he was doing in a way that I could understand. I don't always understand the technical terms that you use."

"No, I guess you wouldn't." Breck was distracted. "Neasa? That restaurant owner?"

"Him? What about Mr. Daniels?"

"Did you know that his father was in the mafia?"

Neasa paled. "No. I had no idea. Was he?"

"That's what Dallas is working on right now. If he is, Neasa, I don't know what we'll do."

Neasa took one look at Breck and then was on her feet, moving quickly from the room and towards the lobby. She stopped to stare out of the door before she sighed. I need to quit running, don't I, Lord? Only I don't know how to.

Chapter 18

Guenivere stood and watched for a moment before she walked towards Neasa, the sound of her footsteps alerting Neasa to the fact that she was not alone. The two ladies stood for a moment, gazing out of the window before Neasa spoke.

"How do I do it, Guenivere? How do I do it? I think I've brought danger to Breck." Neasa's voice was barely a whisper.

"By trusting God, first of all. By trusting Breck. He's been around the block as they say. He'll do everything that he can to keep you safe. So will our guys. And Dallas and the police will as well."

"I get that, Guenivere. But how do I allow that to happen? I don't think I can." Neasa moved to sit in one of the chairs, Guenivere sitting near her.

"It's hard, Neasa. All of us have wanted to run and not put our guys in danger. Some of us married to keep each other safe. Berneen married Baird to save his life. It's who we are, Neasa. That's what we do for one another. It's part of being a family. As Breck's lady, you're part of it now."

"I know." Neasa's voice was still only a whisper. "I just don't know if I can live with myself if something happens to him."

"I don't think that matters to him, Neasa. He's indicated that he wants to be in your life, hasn't he?"

At Neasa's nod, Guenivere reached for her hand, bending her head to pray for her new friend.

Breck stood and watched before he turned back towards the conference room. No, he decided, Neasa needs me. Not the guys. They can work on it well enough on their own. He walked quietly to where she sat, crouching down beside her, an arm around him. He was surprised that she hadn't jumped when he touched her.

"Thank you, Guenivere. Neasa?" Breck watched her profile.

"I'm okay, Breck. Guenivere has helped. Thank you." Neasa gave a small smile, receiving a wide warm one in return from Guenivere. "I've never had friends such as you ladies are to one another."

"We can rectify that, Neasa. We meet on Monday morning for Bible study and prayer. We'll all off on Monday morning. Join us. We try and meet once a week with all of us. And then we pair off. I would like to pair off with you. I usually meet with Fynn. She would welcome you."

"I'll think about it. Right now, I think I need to apologize to a few fellows." Neasa turned as Breck shook his head

"Not needed, Neasa. I did for you. They understand better than you think."

"I know that, Breck." Neasa was frustrated. "What all have they discovered?"

"That Daniels was indeed a criminal and that his restaurant was a front for multiple crime deals. You

—

were fortunate or protected, I should say, that you were only in the kitchen. That's why the staff kept changing. They would only work for a few weeks and then be made to leave in case they saw something. The waitress? Dallas has done some preliminary work on that. The feeling is that she overheard something and that they realized she had. You were the only one to speak with her that day. That's why they are after you. They think she may have said something to her."

"But she didn't. She just left. We all looked at one another after she did and went right back to what we were doing." Neasa leaned against him. "How do I get that message out?"

"I'm not sure that we can, Neasa. They are working to find enough evidence to arrest them. But for now the police there have asked Dallas to make sure that you stay safe."

"And just how do I do that?" Neasa struggled in his arms for a moment before she relaxed. "I don't want anyone hurt. Certainly not the little ones. And that's what they will do."

"We all know that, Neasa. They won't go after anyone but you, or me now that we've been seen together. They won't go after your family. It's not their code."

Neasa was not comforted, not at all, she thought. How do I do this, Lord? How do I begin to date, when I'm in such danger? How to I keep Breck safe?

—

Chapter 19

Dan watched his daughter closely the next morning from where he stood just inside the church doors, Nevin walking towards her. He shook his head. Breck certainly was not who he would have chosen for her. He searched his mind for someone he could send her way and then nodded. He had the perfect candidate. He would talk with him later this afternoon. Dan felt that he had to get Neasa away from Breck, that he was bringing danger to her.

Nevin grinned at his sister as he reached to hug her, finding her moving closer to Breck when he released her.

"How are you, Neasa?"

"Just fine. You?" Her eyes narrowed as she studied her brother. "Nevin?"

"I'm fine, sis. Just fine. Breck?"

"Nevin?" Breck copied the inflection in Nevin's tone, causing the younger man to grin at him. "I see you're on your own."

"I am. Sarah couldn't make it this morning. She's not feeling great."

"Oh, no! What can I do for her?" Neasa's thoughts went to her brother's wife.

"She'll be fine, sis. Just fine. She's been fighting a migraine the last couple of days and thought it best just to stay home. Call her later. She'd like to talk with you."

"I'll do that." Neasa bit at her lip, a habit that Nevin recognized.

"Sis?"

"Nevin? Has anyone been around you, asking about me?"

Nevin shared a look with Breck, who nodded. "No, they haven't. Sarah hasn't mentioned anything either. Now, Dad?" Nevin turned towards the church. "I'm not sure if he would say."

"Not likely." Neasa moved forward as Breck did, heading into the church. "Where do you normally sit?"

"At the back. Is that okay?" Breck suddenly grew hesitant about his normal seat.

"No, that's where I like to sit. Nevin?"

"I'm ushering today, sis. Catch you later." Nevin's steps slowed as he walked towards his father. "Dad?"

"Nevin? How is she?"

"She's fine and she's happy, Dad. Don't do anything to spoil that for her." Nevin walked past his father, suddenly feeling that Sarah had been right. That Dan would do just that, find someone to interfere in Neasa's budding romance. His phone was out as he sent Breck a text, warning him of that.

Buckley and Locklin slid in beside them, Buckley finding it strange that he was no longer behind the pulpit of the church that he had pastored for so long. Neasa greeted them, and then shifted closer to Breck, a sudden chill running down her back and causing her to shiver. Breck frowned and looked around, not seeing anyone that he didn't recognize.

"You're okay?" He bent his head to whisper to her.

"I am, I think." She looked around. "I just feel uncomfortable, but I need to be here. Does that make sense?"

"Perfect sense, darling. Perfect sense." Breck's attention went back to the front, missing her speculative look at the term of endearment that he had called her.

Locklin leaned over. "He means that, Neasa. He doesn't give endearments to just anyone."

Neasa nodded. "I know. It's just so new. And I'm just so uncertain about things."

"We need to talk. Tomorrow, how be we do lunch? Our meeting will be over by then."

"I would like that. Thank you."

Breck watched late that afternoon from where he stood near the Foundation building entrance, Neasa standing a few feet away from him. He didn't know the younger man who had shown up, asking for Neasa.

Neasa had been hesitant to meet him, her hand reaching for Breck as she went forward. He had stopped just short of where she now stood, a whispered word in her ear.

—

"I'm sorry. I don't know you. You said my Dad sent you?"

"He did. He knew I was looking for a lady to date. He suggested that you would be willing to go out with me." The man, who Neasa knew from her father's work, Phil Evans, had a belligerent look on his face.

"Oh, he did, did he? Sorry. I'm not interested. I would suggest that you leave. And don't return." Neasa turned away, just as Phil reached for her arm, stopping her.

"I'm not done yet, Neasa. You will be going out with me. Starting tonight. So let's go. I have reservations at a local restaurant." He looked up as he heard a low growl and saw Breck standing in front of him. "What's your problem? She's leaving with me."

"For starters, I definitely heard her refuse and then suggest you leave." Breck's eyes saw the security guard on duty standing behind Phil. "There's a security guard there, waiting to help you leave. Besides, Neasa's my lady. We're dating."

"No way. She's mine." Phil's fist was back and driven into Breck's jaw without warning, sending Breck flying backward to lie still.

Neasa screamed and then fled to where Breck lay, on her knees, trying to raise his upper body. The guard prevented Phil from moving, handcuffs clicking around his wrists despite his struggles and protests.

Brady was there, on his knees, his hands gentle on Breck's face. He hadn't seen what had transpired, just heard Neasa's scream as he and Fynn were heading out for a drive.

"Neasa?"

"He sucker-punched him, Brady. Oh, what did Dad do?" She looked up, anger sparking in her eyes. "Dad sent him. I refused to go with him and he took offence at that. Breck asked him to leave and that's when he punched him."

Breck's groan had her eyes on him and then her hands on his face. "Breck? Oh, are you okay? Breck?"

"Give him a chance to answer, Neasa." Amusement traced through Brady's words. "It's not broken, but it will be bruised and sore."

Breck sat up, Neasa's arms around him, and stared at Phil. The patrol officer who had responded approached him, crouching down to speak with him.

"You're okay, Breck?"

"I am. Get him out of here. I'm not sure if I'll lay charges or not."

"It's too late. He's been charged with trespassing. He was asked to leave and didn't. That's can't be changed for now. Let him stew in jail for a few hours. He's known for tricks like this." He turned to Neasa. "You're okay?"

"I am. Just so angry. Go and talk to my father. He's the one who caused this. I'm not sure that I can ever face him again."

—

Chapter 20

Dan's face paled as he faced Barnabas who stood on his porch. He shook his head. No, that wasn't what had happened.

"Phil showed up, Dan." Barnabas repeated himself. "He tried to forced Neasa to leave with him even after she had refused. Breck stepped in and Dan punched him, knocking him down and out. Phil has been arrested for trespass because he refused to leave. He may well be charged with assault."

"No, that's not what happened. He called me from jail, asking me to post bond for him. He said Breck attacked him."

"No, that isn't. The security guard on duty was there, making his rounds, and saw it. We also have it on our security feed, which we have turned over to the investigating officer. At the moment, Neasa is refusing to leave the building or the property, which is her right to do so. That is her home at present." Barnabas was frustrated. How had his father's friend sunk to this? "And if case you didn't know it, Breck and Neasa are dating. If you try anything like this again, I will go to the church board and we will be speaking with you. She is an adult, capable of making her own decisions."

"We'll see about that. I'll be out to speak with her." Dan moved to shut the front door, stopping as Barnabas held out a paper.

"I'm sorry, Dan, that it had to come to this. This is a restraining order that Neasa took out against you. You cannot come on to the Foundation grounds. Not at present. In fact, you cannot be in touch with her. This order is directed at you alone. Not your wife. Not your son." Barnabas turned and walked away, sadness in his heart. How did this happen, Lord? And how do we help heal this relationship? It will never be the same, that much I know.

Neasa thrust her phone at Breck, fear on her face. He took it before he looked down at it.

"Your Dad? He's that angry?"

"He is. I've never seen him like that. Barnabas said he'd talk to him, hand him the restraining order. I didn't think that I had any choice." Tears sparkled in her eyes. "Breck?"

Breck simply swept her close to his heart. "I've got you, darling. I've got you. Let your Dad cool off. Bruce and Will I know are intending to speak with him." He turned to her phone again. "It's Nevin."

"Just send him a message. Let him know I'm okay and that I had to."

"Wait. He's downstairs. Stay put, darling. I'll be right back." Breck had taken Neasa to Doc and Anna, Doc examining his jaw and then just shaking his head.

Nevin turned as he heard footsteps and then reached to shake Breck's hand.

"I'm sorry, Breck. I wondered if Dad would be up to something. He can be restrictive with Neasa. That's part of the reason that she moved away. He just doesn't understand that she's an adult and can make her own decisions."

Breck nodded. "I know. She just doesn't need this right now, not with being threatened and followed."

"I wondered. She seemed edgy this morning. She not likely will want to talk to me. Will you tell her that I love her and that I will do everything I can to make sure Dad doesn't try a stunt like this again?"

"I will. Give her a day or so and then call her. Just send her a text later telling her that. She needs your support."

"She has it. Mine and Sarah's." Nevin looked down at the bag that he was holding. "Sarah heard what happened and sent this. A care package if you like. Some of her favourite treats and her hot chocolate."

Breck took the bag, a sad smile on his face. "I'll do that. Thank your Sarah for me." He watched Nevin walk away, hearing footsteps approaching him.

"You okay, Breck?" Benen spoke from beside him, Blair on his other side.

"I am, fellows. Thanks. Where is everyone?"

"Out and about, doing fun stuff. We had just come back when we heard. Nevin okay?" Blair nodded towards the doors.

"He will be. He's hurting for his sister."

"He will. Now, we just need to solve your adventure, you two can marry, and that will be the answer." Benen grinned as he waved and walked away.

———

"Did he really just say that?" Breck stared after him,

"He did, Breck. We can all see your heart. You're not hiding it very well. You are in our prayers." Blair walked away as well, leaving Breck standing staring outside, a frown on his face, a thought crossing his mind that had him shaking his head.

—

Chapter 21

Screaming, Neasa ran for the building, her heart racing in fear even as her feet pounded along the gravel pathway. She could hear the thudding of footsteps getting closer, and that lent wings to her feet. I can do this, she prayed. I see the end of the path. There has to be someone around. Her breath caught in her throat and her chest hurt from the exertion. Just a few more steps, but she didn't make it. Tackled and taken to the ground, Neasa struggled against the man holding her down.

"What did she say?" His guttural voice finally made it through her fear.

"I don't know. Who?" Sobs shook her body even as she continued to struggle, to no avail.

"The waitress. What did she tell you?"

"Nothing. Let me go!" Neasa screamed again, hoping and praying that someone would hear her.

The man shot a glance towards the building and with a curse, his hand was back and then thudding harshly against Neasa's temple, sending her spiraling down into darkness. She lay limp even as he shoved away from her and ran himself, heading back towards the woods and safety.

Brendon ran after him even as Branigan and Brody dropped down beside Neasa.

"Neasa?" Brod tried to rouse her. "She's out cold."

"She is. Is Doc around?"

"No, and neither is Brady. Cadee was but she was heading into town, for a class she said when I saw her earlier."

Branigan nodded, frustration at not having help for Neasa at hand. "Call it in, Brody." He ran back to the building, heading for the infirmary and unlocking it to reach for a folded metal emergency blanket. The door locked behind him, he ran again for the lobby, finding Blair and Bradon standing watching him.

"Branigan?"

"Neasa was attacked. We didn't get there in time." He continued to run, heading for Neasa, shaking out the blanket and wrapping it around her. "Has she roused?"

"No, not at all. Breck's not here?" Blair looked around.

"No, he had meetings out of town today. He thought he would be back about now."

The men stood back as the paramedics arrived and then the patrol officers.

"What happened?"

"We're not sure. We heard Neasa scream and ran this way. We found her like this. Brendon took off towards the woods." Branigan looked around. "Here he is."

Barnabas met Breck as he walked towards the building, pointing towards his truck.

"In, Breck."

"Barnabas? I just got home." Breck protested.

"I know. Neasa's been hurt, about thirty minutes ago. I need to take you to her. They're asking for you. She was awake long enough to name you as her next of kin at the hospital. Did you know that?"

Breck stared at Barnabas. "No. I mean, we talked about it, but I didn't know that she had done that." His head went back as he prayed for his lady. "How bad?"

"Branigan and Brody weren't sure. She has facial bruising, Brody said, that was starting. It looked as if she was hit with something."

Breck's head went back on the headrest as his eyes closed. "Was she outside?"

"She was. She was heading back from the gardens. Brendon took off for the woods but couldn't find anyone. He heard a car pulling away before he got there."

"They've tracked her down. How do I keep her safe? I have to travel. I have meetings."

"I know, Breck. I know. We'll work on what we can, do video conferencing if possible." Barnabas' heart hurt for his friend.

Breck's head shot up. "Her father? If someone has called him, there will be problems."

"I know. I have been praying that didn't happen, but I'm sure it has. Security said for you to head in through the ambulance bay." Barnabas paused his truck long enough for Breck to jump out before he pulled away and into a parking spot, running for the main Emergency Department doors. Blair met him, an angry look on his face.

"Blair?" Barnabas drew him aside, even as he heard the angry raised voice.

"Her father. Some nurse called him. She didn't wait to verify the next of kin. Doc has refused to let him in. Nevin is listed after Breck. She was awake again and adamant about that, as much as she can talk. Dan's not taking it well." Blair turned to watch the older man. "What is his problem, anyway?"

"That's what we need to find out. Did someone call it in?"

"Security did. Will is on his way. So is Dallas. He's worried about Breck. They received another threat today, this time from someone on the street. Breck's been targeted too." Blair blew out a breath.

"Of course he has been. Listen, Breck went in through the ambulance bay. Doc called and asked for that. We need to keep him out of sight of Dan until Dan is removed." Barnabas looked around as he felt a hand on his shoulder. "Dad?"

"Will called. First, Neasa?" Bruce was concerned about Breck's lady.

"I don't know yet, Dad. She has been awake on and off from what Blair has said. This is the problem that we need to deal with."

Bruce's hand kept his son in place. "We don't. Barnabas, this time we let the authorities deal with him. I hate to say it, but he's changed in the last year or so. He has always had a temper but has been able to keep it under control. I think that is part of why Neasa left home. Nevin has come to me and talked over the years."

"He has? And it could be."

Chapter 22

Doc met Breck as he headed down the hall towards the desk, reaching for his arm and pulling him into an empty examination room.

"Doc? Neasa?"

"She's in imaging right now, son. She took a blow to her face. I want to ensure that she doesn't have a fracture."

Breck sank back against the wall. "Her face? It was that hard a blow?" At Doc's nod, Breck scrubbed at his face with his hands. "How long will she be?"

Doc glanced at the clock. "She should be back in a couple of minutes. But there is a situation that you need to be aware of. One of the nurses didn't listen to who Neasa said was her next of kin and called her father."

"No! And he has a restraining order against him from her. Make sure that nurse understands that."

"Oh, she has been told. She's in her supervisor's office right now. It's not the first complaint against her." Doc's hand rested on Breck's shoulder. "I was told that Dan showed up and was fighting with the security guards. They called in the police."

"And that will not go over well. Can I see her?"

"Wait here. I'll be back." Doc was back shortly. "Come with me, Breck. She's this way."

Without any hesitation, Breck walked up to the stretcher, his eyes on Neasa. He grimaced as he saw the spreading bruise that started on her temple. A hand reached for hers, finding her cold, but her fingers tightened on his. She stirred, not quite waking, before she was still again. As best he could with one hand, Breck tucked the blankets around her, before he just stood, watching his lady, wishing that it was him lying there and not her.

Barnabas paused in the doorway, an hour later, as he watched his friend. Doc had finally made Breck sit, telling him that he needed to. Breck had nodded, not taking his eyes away from Neasa as Doc explained their findings. He had sighed, asked if she was being admitted, and was adamant that he was not leaving her. Doc had nodded, said he would make that possible, and had walked away after praying for the couple.

"Breck?" Barnabas' quiet voice broke into Breck's thoughts and he looked around.

"You're here?"

"Of course, I am. We all are. No one will leave until they hear from you how Neasa is. You know our group."

Breck nodded, exhaustion seeping through him. "No fractures, thank God. Doc doesn't think a concussion but he can't rule it out. She's been up and down for the last little while."

"They're keeping her in?"

"Doc wants to, but there's a bed shortage right now. I want to take her home, Barnabas. Anna sent word for us to come to them."

"And Cadee and Brady have volunteered to help." Barnabas leaned against the end of the bed. "Has Neasa been awake long enough to say what happened?"

"Just enough to give a statement. And it wasn't all that clear. She was attacked as she ran from the gardens. She didn't get a look at the man. All he asked was what the waitress had said."

"So, it is what we thought."

Breck nodded, standing to place his hand against Neasa's cheek as she moved restlessly. "It is. You're staying?"

"I will. I'll be out in the waiting room. I'll send the others home." He handed over a bag. "Cadee brought in some clothes for Neasa, that would be easy for her to put on, she said."

"Cadee is such a compassionate caring person. Thank her for me." Breck paused. "Neasa's father?"

"Unfortunately, he was arrested. He assaulted a security guard and also a police officer. I have no idea what's going on with him. Neither does Dad or Will."

"Nevin called. He said his father's temper got worse after Neasa left home. Why, he couldn't say." Breck's hand rested against the uninjured side of Neasa's face. "Take us home, Barnabas. That's where we need to be."

"I will. I'll send Doc in. He's figuring that's what you would want."

Chapter 23

Neasa shifted restlessly, not quite asleep, not quite awake, in the early morning hours. She felt arms tighten around her and shifted again to peer through pain-filled eyes. She knew this place, she thought before she snuggled down against whoever it was that was holding her and slept, a natural sleep this time.

Breck's head rested against Neasa as he slept, holding the love of his life, he had decided, as he sat in a comfortable armchair in Doc's living room. Anna had covered the two of them and then sat in her own chair, watching. She had sent Doc off to bed, knowing that he needed the sleep, with the promise to rouse him if she needed to. She prayed for her young friends, suddenly fearful for them, and then had shaken her head. Breck had been reluctant to leave the night before and Neasa just refused to let go of him, muttering that he kept her safe and that he couldn't leave her.

Breck finally roused in the early morning hours and looked around before he yawned and rubbed at his face. His eyes went to Neasa and he smiled before he rose and headed for the bedroom Anna had prepared for her, tucking her into bed and then leaving, closing the door behind him. He left the apartment quietly, heading for his own, to shower and shave and change. The ringing of his phone distracted him as he stood for a moment in his office and he reached for it.

"Dad? You're calling? I didn't think that you would!"

"Breck, son? Are you okay? Your mother and I have had such a burden for you. I headed out last night to where I could find service. We're planning on heading home in the next week or so."

"You are? Wonderful? Me? I'm okay, I guess."

"I don't like that hesitation." Beck Curran knew his son well.

"It's like this, Dad. I came to the rescue of a beautiful lady and have found my love."

Beck stared at his phone before he began to laugh. "You did and you have? You're off on one of those adventures like the others?"

"We are, Dad. I won't go into all the details but she is in danger. Right now, she's with Anna and Doc. She was hurt last night."

"She was? Your Mom and I will be praying. In fact, she made me promise to tell you that. She's had such a burden the last couple of weeks."

"It's been about that long. Neasa really needs our prayers. She's struggling with some other stuff as well."

"Neasa? Dan's Neasa? Oh, Breck, what have you done?" Beck hesitated before saying anything.

"Dad? I don't like the sounds of that?"

"No, I didn't think you would. Listen, I'm running low on charge. I'll talk with you when we get back. Just watch yourself around Dan. He can come across as jovial and happy but there is a dark side to him that not many see. I am afraid that you will."

"We have, Dad. We have. Give Mom my love. You're flying back when?"

"Knowing your mother, likely in the next day or so. We have accomplished what we needed to here in the village and can head home at any time. The people here are growing so fast in the Lord."

"Oh, that's great, Dad. Don't cut it short because of me."

"We're not. God has been nudging us to leave the last few days."

Breck stared at his phone before he tucked it into his pocket. His parents, Beck and Bonnie, were on their way home. He couldn't wait for Neasa to meet them. He reached for the flowers that he had had Berneen pick up for him the night before and headed back for Doc's, finding Anna waiting for him.

"Anna?" Breck looked past her.

"It's okay, Breck. She roused and couldn't find you. I managed to calm her down. Do you realize how much she needs you?"

"I do, Anna. I do. And I need her." He reached to hug Anna. "I spoke with Dad this morning."

"You did? I didn't think that they had cell service." Anna bustled around the kitchen, preparing their breakfast, her heart raised in prayer for all of the building as she did so.

"He came out to where he could get service. They'll be home in a couple of days."

"That's early." Doc stood in the doorway.

"It is, Doc. But Dad says they've accomplished what they felt they needed to and are free to come home." Breck took the mug of coffee offered to him and then leaned against the counter.

"Good. You need him here with you." Doc hesitated before he spoke. "Neasa's mother?"

"She's still away. Nevin was unclear when she would be coming home. It's almost as if he was afraid to say that she wasn't."

"I see." Doc laid a hand on Breck's shoulder for a moment. "We're praying for them all."

"Thanks, Doc." Breck's mug hit the counter as he heard a whisper of sound from the hall and headed that way, finding Neasa there, turning in a circle, her hand to her head. "Neasa?"

"Breck? You're here. I dreamt that you left me." She launched herself at his open arms, her own around his neck. "Don't leave me, Breck. Please don't leave me."

Chapter 24

Three days later, Neasa wandered her apartment, restless but not sure what she should be doing. She was afraid to leave the building, and then grew angry with herself. That was not the way she wanted to live, she decided, and reached for her shoes and a jacket, heading for the stairs. A hand on her head, Neasa walked towards the doors, hesitating before she walked outside and then around the building, slower than she normally. Paul, the security guard on duty, followed her from a distance.

Neasa paused, turning her face up to the sun, feeling the warmth from it even though the air was chilly. This is my favourite time of year, she thought, a time to head into a season of rest and recuperation. And I need that, don't I, Lord? I am afraid to love, to let go and let Breck totally into my heart. He's the one, isn't he, Lord? He's the one that You planned for me. I see that, but I am just so afraid. Teach me how to love again, Lord. Somewhere over the years, that disappeared. I say the words but I don't feel them in my heart. And that is not how it is to be.

Breck watched her for a moment before he moved towards her, his footsteps spinning her around, fear momentarily on her face. He simply stopped, arms open as she ran towards him, launching herself into them. He stood, the most precious bit of lady in his arms, he thought, feeling as she hugged him back hard.

Something had changed, Breck thought. I wonder what.

"You're back, Breck. I didn't expect you until later." Neasa looked back, a happy look on her face. "I was afraid for you today."

"I know, darling. I was afraid for you. I am so glad that you ventured outside." He watched as a cloud covered her face before it cleared.

"I am taking back my life, Breck. I have been under a cloud or shadow or whatever you want to call it for years. That's why I left, I think, to try and reclaim my life, but that didn't happen."

"But it has now." Breck hugged her again, a kiss on the top of her head. "That warms my heart so much, darling. Care to share?"

Neasa shrugged. "God and I had a conversation a while ago. He just told me to start living and loving. So I am. I am running towards my life once more."

"Run towards me?" Breck drew in his breath. Did he really say that?

"If you want me to, I intend to." Neasa studied him, seeing the relief on his face.

"I do, Neasa, my darling. I do. I want to walk through life with you by my side." He turned her, his arm around her. "We'll talk, but first I have someone or two someones who want to meet you, very much."

"You do?" Neasa's steps slowed for a moment. "Oh! Your parents! I have met your mother. We were part of a Bible study until I left. She's so sweet."

"Mom said that she knew you, but not as my lady." Breck grinned down at her even as he felt eyes on him. He refused to look around, not wanting to give satisfaction to the watcher. But he would be out later, when it was still light, to have a look around.

Beck and Bonnie watched as the younger couple walked towards them, arms around one another.

"He's found his lady, Bonnie." Beck spoke quietly, not sure why that was.

"He has. I often wondered if she would be the one. She seemed to suit him." Bonnie reached for Neasa's hands before she simply swept her into a tight hug. "Neasa. Welcome to the family. We've been waiting for you for so long."

"You have?" Neasa stood back, her hands still in Bonnie's. "Tell me something. Is everyone in your family so open and honest, Breck?"

Breck began to grin. "You'll find Mom is. And she's right, darling. We have been waiting for a long time. All my life, in fact."

Beck began to laugh before he reached to hug Neasa as well. "That we have, Neasa. Now, let me take you all out for supper somewhere. Bonnie and I have been hungry for a good burger and fries."

"Dad has spoken, Neasa, but it's your choice." Breck and his father shared a look, Beck nodding at Breck's words.

"That it is, Neasa. We will not force you to go, but we would like it very much if you did join us."

"I'm dangerous to be around, Beck, Bonnie. Someone is after me." Neasa was suddenly afraid to do just that.

"We'll take precautions, love." Bonnie had her arm around Neasa, leading her towards the parking lot. "I could use some girl support. These two men of ours tend to ignore me."

"Not all the time, Mom." Breck laughed at his mother's comment.

"No, not all the time, but you and your father can get into discussions that I can't join in. Not that I mind." She winked at Neasa who suddenly broke out into laughter.

"Bonnie, you have no idea how much you have just helped me." Neasa quickened her pace. "Who's driving?"

Chapter 25

Breck stared down at his desk the next day, his thoughts not really on the work piled there before he reached for a folder. His thoughts were on Neasa and his parents, and his smile grew. She had teased his father, stuck up for his mother, and just listened as they had talked about where they had been. She had asked all the right questions, he thought, not just from politeness but from genuine interest. His father had nodded at him at the end of the evening, giving his approval for Breck's choice.

His thoughts coming back to his work, Breck steadily made his way through the evaluations of the twelve men that were employed by the Foundation. It wasn't necessary, he thought, to do these, but each man had asked that it be done, just in fairness to both sides. He found no complaints from any of the men. In fact, Breck thought, the men thought that they were being given too much. He smiled at that thought. God had led Barnabas to each of the men and that showed in their character.

His phone ringing disturbed him and he absentmindedly answered it, his full attention coming to the call as he heard Dallas' voice.

"Breck? Where are you?"

"In my office. Why?"

"Because I need you to stay there. Neasa?"

"She's with Mom and Dad, I think. They were heading this way earlier today." Breck was on his feet, heading for the door as it opened and the three appeared. "Actually, they're here with me now."

"Stay in your office. Lock yourselves in. I'm on my way with patrol officers. There's been a threat made against you directly today, Breck, and it states that they will hit the building to get to you."

Breck paled even as he reached for his lady, to wrap her under an arm. "Today?"

"Today. Stay put." Dallas cut off the call, heading for the Foundation building. Will had approached him just moments before, a grim look on his face, as he handed over the paperwork Dallas had given him.

"Find Breck. Dan is out and on the hunt for Breck. He's managed to find a couple of men to go with him. They're heading for the Foundation building, fully intending on harming Breck and bringing Neasa home."

"That would be kidnapping."

Will nodded. "It would be but they're trying to play it that she is mentally unsound. I know the men. They will not stop at violence to take her."

Dallas nodded, before he ran for his car, hearing Will call that he had ordered patrol vehicles to head that way.

Breck answered the knock on his door an hour later to find both Dallas and Barnabas standing there. He stepped back to let them enter, the door closing behind them before he moved to where Neasa had seated herself.

"Dallas? Barnabas?" Breck looked between the two men.

"I'm sorry, Neasa. It was your father. He was heading this way with two men to bring you back to his home." Dallas' face was still grim.

"He was? He just doesn't let go? What will it take to make him? I tried moving away and even that didn't work out so well." Neasa blinked back tears of hurt, Breck's arm around her.

"We don't know, Neasa. This time, we have arrested your father with charges of threatening death, conspiracy, and attempted kidnapping. He'll have a high bail to make."

"He'll make it. He'll have friends who will." Neasa watched Dallas closely. "Let me guess. He's tried to declare me incompetent."

"He has, Neasa. We're working on fighting those charges."

"So, what do I do to help that? Be out and about and put everyone in danger?"

"That will help. We need you and Breck to be seen together more than you have been." Barnabas took up the conversation. He held up a hand as she protested. "I know, Neasa. It's putting both of you at risk, but we need to do something. Dallas has information that he's working on regarding the restaurant owner. In fact, he has spoken with the police in that city and the man is under arrest. He understands that you did not speak to the waitress or have any information regarding him. He has agreed to call off whoever it was that he sent after you."

"When?"

"I'm sorry." Dallas frowned. "What do you mean?"

"When did he do that?"

"A week ago?"

"Then who was it who attacked me and asked that? There has to be someone. I'm not safe, not until we find that person."

"And the fellows are working away on that. There hasn't been a lot that they have discovered yet. Brady has reached out to a friend."

"A friend? And just who would that be?"

"A lady named Emma. She finds people and information that no one else seems to be able to."

"I know an Emma who does that. She has a little boy named Isaac."

Breck's arm tightened on Neasa. "That is Emma. Once she knew it was for you, she dropped what she was working on and started on that investigation."

"She did? That sounds like her. I know her and Abe's story. It wasn't pretty." Neasa leaned suddenly against Breck. "I'm tired, Breck. Can I go home?" Her eyes closed as she slept.

Breck stared down at her before his mother spoke.

“She’s been pushing too hard for too many years, son. Now that she feels safe with you, she’s relaxing. And this is part of it.”

Chapter 26

Breck turned from the window that he had been staring out in Barnabas' office, waiting until his friend was finished with his telephone call. He had heard Barnabas' steps behind him.

"Barnabas?"

"Breck? Has Dallas been back in touch?"

Breck shook his head. "Not since we spoke this morning. Neasa went with my parents for the day. She's hurting, Barnabas, and I don't know how to make it better."

"Has she spoken with her mother?" Barnabas leaned against the door frame to the office hallway.

"Not that I know of. She's leery to do that, she said, just in case her mother is involved."

"Do you think she is?" Barnabas watched him closely.

Breck shrugged. "At this point in time? I have no idea. Neither does Nevin. Nevin is hurting for his sister and for himself. Sarah is trying to keep his spirits up, he said, but it's tough."

"It is. Would Neasa speak with Ker? She might be able to help, given what happened with her mother."

"I have asked Neasa, but she is not ready to do that, she said. Maybe at some point. I did, just to try and get a sense of what I can do to help Neasa."

"Good. Talk with Buckley as well, even though I know you have." Barnabas shoved away from the door frame. "Have you been to the conference room?"

"Not today. I've been swamped with paperwork and then phone calls." Breck sighed, rubbing at his temple with one finger. "I have no idea how the fellows did this."

"With a lot of prayer and support." Barnabas' hand rested on Breck's shoulder as he prayed for his friend. "Now, let's head for the conference room, see what they can tell us, and then you need to head to find your lady."

The twelve men looked up as Breck entered, waving, or calling out a greeting. They had been in there since early that afternoon and were planning on breaking off soon. They watched Breck closely, seeing the strain in him that they all recognized.

Breck walked the room, studying the whiteboards, reaching for a marker to add his own comments, before he stood back, nodding. They were working well again, he thought, finding information that he had not even dreamed was out there. His head turned as Benen stopped beside him.

"Breck? How are you?"

Breck shrugged. "About how you all were at this point. I'm afraid for Neasa, but I'm not sure why or who from."

"We know that, Breck. Dallas has been around. He said you told him to talk with us, and he did. We have that information. Emma is starting to feed us information on her friend, Neasa." Benen slanted a glance at Breck.

Breck grinned. "I just found out this morning that Neasa is acquainted with a little guy who has parents named Emma and Abe. I don't know how or when they met, but Emma has been a friend to Neasa from what she said."

"I'm sure that she has been." Benen looked down at the floor, not sure how to continue. "Her father?"

"Dan? It's strange, you know, how he is reacting. Nevin has been talking with me. I can't say what all he said, but he did tell me that this goes way back to before Neasa ever left home."

"It is bizarre. To try and kidnap her? I know right well he's going to claim that she's incompetent."

"We know that. We're working on some plans. No, not marrying like some of you. Not yet." Breck thought back to his conversation with his lady. She had not wanted to make that move, not ready for it yet.

"No, she's not. Neither are you. When those of us did that, we were ready. The ladies understood why and agreed."

"That they did. Listen, I have to run. I'll be back. Make sure you fellows pack it in soon." Breck walked away, not seeing twelve pairs of eyes watching him before they exchanged glances.

"How do we do it, fellows?" Branigan spoke up. "He was there for each of us. How do we do it for him?"

"Keep plugging away at this." Bradon pointed to his computer and then the papers stacked by each man. "Find the one responsible and bring him or her to justice. And we know it could be a woman just as easily."

Baird raised his head at that. "That fellow who had the restaurant? Did we ever find anything on his wife or daughter?"

"Not yet, but we're still digging." Burnie rose and stretched. "Sorry, fellows. I need to run. Muir and Granny are expecting me for dinner and it's almost that time."

Chapter 27

Breck paced the next morning, his phone to his ear, as he listened to the police detective from another town speak with him. He sighed to himself. This is not what he needed. One of the properties that the Foundation had been looking into buying had been damaged in a fire. He had been the name that had been given to contact.

"It's a total loss?"

"It is, Mr. Curran. I'm sorry. I know that you were in the planning stages of purchasing it."

"Any chance that it was accidental?"

"No. Our arson dog hit a number of spots where accelerants were used. It is definitely arson. We'll be working with the arson investigator on it. We'll ensure that you are kept abreast of what we find."

"Thank you." Breck tossed his phone to the desk. Now what, Lord? That was a big project that just got put on hold. He would need to bring a report to the board and right away. He dropped to his desk chair and sent off a group email, detailing what he had been told. He then sat back, a frown on his face. That property was where he had been just a few days ago. Had he been followed and someone did this as a warning to him or Neasa?

Bruce turned as Barnabas gave an exclamation, frowning.

"Son?"

"Breck just sent out a group email. The property in Purdy? It was destroyed in an arson fire."

"Arson? And Breck was just there? Any connection?" Bruce watched his son closely.

"I wonder if there is. A threat against him, perhaps? Or it could just be coincidental." Barnabas sat back in his chair. "He's hurting, Dad, and for the first time in our friendship, I don't know what to say to him or how to help him."

"Praying for him helps. Just standing beside him is what you can do. You have always done that." Bruce paused, his mind going back to the two men, watching them grow in his mind. "You two have had disagreements but nothing that ever came between you. He's moving on to a new aspect of his life, Barnabas, that he will not be sharing with you. That breaks a portion of your friendship. I mean, you two will always be friends, but it's changing and growing."

"I know, Dad. Breck and I have often spoken of what would happen if and when we ever met our ladies. He has. Neasa completes his heart, as he has often said he wanted. Just how do we keep them safe? That's a question that I don't have an answer for."

"None of us do. Tell me where your men stand right now in their investigation."

"Nowhere near finding out who it is. We've ruled out the restaurant owner. He had no idea that Neasa was the cook or that the waitress may have heard something. He's under arrest for other things. We're looking at his wife and daughter. He has no son, contrary to what Neasa was led to believe."

"Then, who was it that pretended to be the son?"

"Emma's working on that. She and Neasa are friends. I have no idea how they met but it helps. She's starting to feed us bits and pieces as she can."

"Good. She's a wonder, that lady. And has quite the story to tell, from what she has said. I've had talks with her and Abe."

"You have? I wasn't aware that you had even met her."

"I meet many people during the course of a year. Now, about Breck? Is he okay for staff in his office? I know his secretary was off for her cancer treatments."

"Becky? She has been. Breck said that she was putting in her resignation. She doesn't feel that she wants to continue to work, even though she enjoys the work. We'll be looking to replace her. He's been working without a secretary for now."

"Neasa? What is she planning? I know she's a chef but is hesitant to continue. That much she has told me, when we've talked. And we've had many conversations, that young lady and me. Would she be willing to step in for a bit?"

Barnabas shrugged. "I can ask, but somehow I don't think so." He looked up as Amy tapped at his door.

"Sorry to interrupt, but Neasa is here. She would like to speak with both of you. She wasn't aware that

Bruce was here, but her face lit up when she found out he was.”

“Of course, Amy.” Barnabas was on his feet, heading for the reception area, watching Neasa as she shifted from foot to foot. “Neasa? I wasn’t expecting to see you today but come in. Dad and I were just talking.”

“Thank you, Barnabas. I really do need to speak with the two of you.” Neasa was edgy and upset, that the two men could tell.

“Neasa? What can we do for you?” Bruce shared a look with Barnabas.

“This.” Neasa thrust an envelope towards him. “This came. Someone has made a complaint that I am incompetent and that I need to report for an assessment to a mental health ward.”

“What!” Bruce took the letter and read it. “You do nothing without legal representation, Neasa. Let me speak with John, one of our lawyers. You stay put. Barnabas, find Breck, and get him here.”

———

Chapter 28

Neasa sat back, drawing in a deep breath, relieved that someone actually believed her for a change. She had never really felt that with her father. He made the decisions and demanded that she go along. He covered that with a smile when they were out and about, but she still felt under his thumb. Nevin wasn't even aware of all that she had faced. Neasa knew her mother had not yet returned and wondered at that. Was she escaping, Lord? Is that why she's not coming back? I pray for her safety. Nevin will be okay. Dad never treated him like he did me.

She felt an arm around her and leaned back against Breck, knowing he had dropped what he was doing and came to find her. Breck studied her face, seeing the fear and distress in it.

Bruce sat back down, a stern look on his face.

"John is on his way." He tapped the envelope. "He will deal with this. He did have a suggestion, Breck, and I will not push you to it."

"I know, Bruce. That we marry. I can't do that to Neasa. She needs this time."

Neasa had turned to watch Breck, seeing his concern for her in his eyes. "Breck? Is that what he will suggest?"

"He might, but then it would be used against you. They would say that you did that just to avoid the assessment." Breck shared another look with Bruce and then Barnabas. "Do we know who instigated it?"

"No. But John will look into it thoroughly. He has his secretary working on it right now. He thought something was up and had already started the process."

"It may be Dad. Is he free?"

"No, he's not. Not yet, Neasa, but his lawyer could be doing something." Bruce pulled out his phone and sent off a text.

John stood for a moment, watching Neasa before his attention turned to Breck. *Bruce is right. He is head over heels in love with his lady, and I can see that she returns that, even if she won't admit it yet.* He sighed. *This notice is not what they need.* He set his briefcase on the floor and reached to shake Breck's hand.

"This is Neasa, John, the reason that you're here." Breck introduced the two.

"Neasa? I've seen you around church. The little ones just love you. My granddaughter is always excited when you're in the children's church."

"Little Abby? Oh, she is such a sweetheart. Loves to cuddle." Her brow clouded. "But what about this?" She pointed to the envelope that Bruce had handed him.

"We'll look at it. I have confirmation that your father's lawyer is the one asking for this. Neasa, have you any idea why?"

Neasa shrugged. "Other than he can't control me any longer? I have no idea. I don't think that I have any money coming to me. At least, not that I am aware of."

"Okay. So, what we do is this. My secretary has already prepared forms for you to sign. We thought this would be coming up. I will go before the courts tomorrow. I have already scheduled it, or my secretary did. I will need you there, both you and Breck." He studied the young couple. "And don't even consider getting married today. That will go bad for you."

"We figured that out, John." Breck grinned for a moment. "We are dating but not that far. Not yet, anyway."

"Okay." John pulled out his phone and then excused himself. He was sober when he returned. "Breck, there has been a new wrinkle. His lawyer has gone to the press, stating that you are holding her here against her will, and that you are poisoning her against her father."

"What!" Breck was on his feet. "You know that's not true."

"We do. I talked to Cindy. She's the lawyer we use in cases like this, Neasa. She has already filed for an injunction against your father, his lawyer, and the press. We would like to do a video statement with you two, to put out there. But it won't go out until after tomorrow's court."

"I see." Neasa wrinkled her brow as she thought, bringing Breck's attention to it. "What if someone is forcing Dad to do this? Has that been looked into?"

Barnabas spoke from where he was standing near the window. "It has been, Neasa. Emma has found evidence of that and sent it on to Dallas. Our fellows had also had that thought and found a person of interest, shall we say, who is pushing your father. We can't say any more than that as it is an active investigation. Dallas has indicated that he plans to speak with you two in the next day or so. This may push him to do that."

Neasa sighed, relaxing back against Breck. "Why? That's all I want to know is why?"

"We don't know yet, Neasa, but we are rushing to discover that. You are still not safe, that much we know." Breck shared a look with Bruce. "I promise to do my best to protect you."

"But they have already hurt you, Breck." She rubbed at her temple, the headache starting to throb.

"You're hurting. John?"

John looked up, his attention on them again. "Neasa? Do you know anyone who would force your father to take this step?"

"No, I don't know his business acquaintances. I mean, I may have seen them but I don't know who they are. I ran the equipment for Dad, that's all. I didn't want to be involved in anything else. How does all this relate to the bones?"

"That's a good question, and I certainly will take it up with Dallas. As of now, young lady, I am your lawyer. Any questions, you send them to me. If you want me to be present when you speak with anyone, call me and I will be there." John gathered up his papers and briefcase and walked away, leaving Neasa staring after him.

"Did he just do that?"

Breck laughed, seeing the humour in it. "He did, Neasa. It's a habit he has. He states what he wants to and then leaves."

"Oh! I thought it was me."

"Never you, darling. Never you."

Chapter 29

The next morning, Neasa sat near the front of the courtroom, watching John as he sat waiting for the judge to appear. Her hand was tight in Breck's and she leaned against him, seeking to find peace and comfort from that contact. Nevin sat on her other side, her hand in his, Sarah beside him. She knew that Barnabas and his parents were there as were Breck's parents. Neasa was still worried. Cindy, the lawyer, had been out the previous night and prepared their video for release. She had smiled at Neasa and told her that the injunctions had been served.

Neasa stood when the judge entered and then re-seated herself, listening carefully to what was being said, not understanding all the legalese. She frowned as the judge nodded, made a comment, and then John approached her.

"Neasa, the judge would like to speak with you. If you are willing to do so and only if you are. He has made that abundantly clear." John shared a look with Breck, who kept his face carefully shuttered. "I think you should, but it's your choice."

"Breck?" Neasa turned to him.

"If John thinks it will help then maybe you should. But as John has stated, it is your choice. The judge will accept that."

———

Neasa stared at the judge, finding a kindly eye directed her way. "I guess then it's okay. Breck, pray for me."

"I am, darling. I am." He stood to let her rise and follow John to the front, moving past the tables to sit near the judge.

"Miss Deakin, thank you for your willingness to speak with me. I will allow questions from the lawyers, but if you are uncomfortable at all, turn to me. I have a few questions that I will ask as well."

Neasa nodded, her eyes on John as he rose. She answered his questions in a quiet, calm voice before her father's lawyer rose, an almost sneer on his face, disbelief, and a bullying manner in his demeanour.

"Miss Deakin, I understand that you were involved in a situation in the city. Were you not?"

"No, sir. I was not."

"Oh, but I have proof. It was regarding a murder of a waitress from the restaurant that you were employed in. You are part of the group that was involved in her murder."

"I'm sorry, sir. I am not. I didn't even know for sure that she had been murdered."

"Oh come, now. Of course, you were. You came back here to hide, didn't you?"

"No, sir, I did not." Neasa was adamant in her answers and she caught a quick look on Breck's face. Oh no, Lord, he's growing angry. Please, Lord? Calm him.

"Move on, Mr. Lawson. She has answered your question." The judge nodded at the lawyer.

"Now, Miss Deakin, regarding this claim. Your father states adamantly that you are incompetent mentally. That you are being held against your will. He wishes a mental health assessment for you. And that happens today."

Neasa's eyes narrowed and she refused to answer.

"Judge, make her answer. She has accusations against her that need to be addressed."

John was on his feet. "Your Honour, I have affidavits here that are signed by everyone who resides in the Foundation building, as well as by her brother and his wife, by the minister of her church, the complete church board. She is not being held against her will. Nor is she incompetent mentally in any way. I have an affidavit from a former forensics psychologist who spoke with her at length yesterday afternoon at my request. Dr. Darcie Foster is well known for her work."

"Dr. Foster? Mr. Lawson, I am denying you this claim of incompetence and being held against her will. You will not appear before this court or any other with these claims. If you do, I will instruct the staff to contact the bar association. This is not the first time that you have tried something like this in one of our courts." He turned to Neasa. "Thank you, Miss Deakin. You are free to go. You will not face any further charges of this sort. Court dismissed." The gavel hit harder than it usually did, showing his displeasure with the lawyer.

Neasa made her way back to Breck, to be enfolded in his arms, before she turned to Nevin and Sarah.

"I'm sorry, Neasa. I didn't know that Dad was like this." Nevin was grieved for his sister.

"It's not your fault, Nevin. You didn't know. Dad wasn't always like this. That's what so strange." Neasa finally made her way out of the courthouse, settling into Breck's truck, his parents in the back seat.

"Are you okay?" Bonnie reached forward to touch her shoulder.

"I am, I think, thank you." Neasa groaned. "That sounded so positive and sure, now didn't it?"

Bonnie gave a soft laugh. "We'll take it as you meant it, Neasa. I was not surprised to have the judge ask for you to speak."

"You weren't?" Neasa twisted to watch her.

"No. He's known for that." Beck smiled at her. "He's done it before. And the lawyer that your father has? One more complaint against him and he's disbarred. He doesn't have a good reputation."

"Then why would Dad pick him?"

"I suspect that he was chosen for your father. We need to find out who is behind it all, Neasa." Breck finally pulled into his parking spot. "Mom, Dad, Anna, and Doc asked that we come to their place."

"We certainly shall. Anna called this morning, to make sure that we would." Bonnie was out of the truck, pulling Neasa with her, heading for the lobby of the building, greeting the men and women who had gathered. "Neasa is free of all that, people. The judge had her speak, told the lawyer off, and let her go."

"Wonderful." Branigan led the cheer that followed, surprising Neasa, who stared at them all before she too grinned.

"It was all your prayers that did it. Thank you." She went from one to the other, thanking them and hugging each one, touching gentle hands to the little ones held in their parents' arms. She laughed at the signs Hailey and Hollie and Darbie were holding. "You three. It's a good thing that you weren't there. I couldn't have kept a straight face."

"We knew you would be okay. God told us that." Hailey hugged her before running off, Hollie on her heels.

Chapter 30

Neasa stretched out on the couch in Doc's living room, her eyes drifting closed. Her head was pounding, she thought, worse than it had been. Even the prescription pain medication that Breck had handed her to take wasn't working. She slept, not hearing the movement, talk and laughter that surrounded her. She felt part of the building family, at last, she thought, just before she slept.

Breck sat where he could watch her, knowing that she had not been sleeping. She had confessed that to him just a while before that. Worry, she said, frustration and pain all contributed to that. It didn't matter how much she prayed, or wanted to move on, to find the love that she needed and craved, she still felt trapped. He prayed for his lady love, praying for her to find the peace that she needed and that she would run to him to find the love that she craved.

He frowned, suddenly on his feet, moving towards her, holding her as her body began to jerk and twitch.

"Doc? Seizure." Breck's sudden loud call broke through the conversation, stilling it abruptly.

"Anna. 9-1-1. Breck, on the floor with her." Doc helped, watching Neasa closely as the seizure stopped. "Has she had these before?"

"No, not that she's said. She did say that her headaches are worse, that even the prescription medication isn't working."

"And has she seen her family doctor?"

"No, not that I know of. She's been too scared to go anywhere the last few days." Breck moved away as the paramedics moved in, his mother's arm around him. He was following the stretcher rapidly as it moved from the apartment and then through the lobby, not seeing the building family had gathered, worry on their face.

Barnabas stepped up to Beck.

"Beck? We heard the sirens. What happened?"

"Neasa had a seizure."

"A seizure? I know she's still been having headaches. Head on in. I'll follow." Barnabas watched them almost run for their car before he turned to the group behind him.

"We need to pray, people. Neasa had a seizure."

Buckley was moving towards the door, Locklin with him. "I'm on my way. I'll update as I can."

Breck paced the waiting room, thinking of how many times that he had done just that. Only this time? It was his lady that was sick and being treated. Dear Lord, please? He could not even put into words his thoughts, but he knew that was just fine. That's when the Spirit prays, isn't it, God?

His parents watched him closely and then turned to Locklin.

"Locklin? The prayer chain is working?"

"I would think so. I called the coordinator on our way in." Locklin was distressed. "I wish sometimes that we were still the minister couple but God had other plans for us."

"He did, dear, and you are where you are needed. God knows that." Bonnie hugged the younger woman. "Now, tell me about this ministry. I haven't had a chance to talk to you or Buckley about it." Bonnie knew about it, had kept up to date on it, but was using this as a tactic to distract Locklin.

Buckley paced beside his friend, his prayers raising for the couple and the medical team.

"I didn't get a chance to talk to you earlier. Everything is okay now with the assessment?"

Breck drew a deep sigh. "It is. The judge was harsh on the lawyer, but he deserved it. Neasa was not to testify but the judge specifically asked her to. It helped that Darcie had talked to her and John had an affidavit from her."

"He did? Oh, wonderful. Darcie is such a caring person. I can't see how that police officer treated her as he did."

Breck turned suddenly as he heard his name called and almost ran towards the nurse waiting for him, leaving Buckley standing and staring after him.

"Breck? This way. Doc has asked that you come." The nurse pointed him into one of the rooms.

Breck was through the door and at Neasa's side almost before the nurse had finished her sentences. His hand reached for hers, as he studying the medical equipment surrounding her, the oxygen mask on her face, the IV line looped and taped to the back of her other hand.

"Doc?" He raised frightened eyes to Doc, finding him standing beside him.

"She's stable right now, Breck. Patrick will be in shortly to speak with you. He's run the bloodwork we needed to, the imagining studies, the tests that he needs to." Doc prayed for his young friend. "He'll have the results for you. Her medication?"

"Here." Breck pulled it from his pocket, a frown on his face. "You know, she hasn't wanted to take it. I gave her one this afternoon, just to see if it would help. I think it's the first one that she had."

"Is that right?" Doc pulled out his reading glasses and studied the medication name. "I'll be back." He was off before Breck could say anything.

Breck turned his attention to Neasa, a hand resting against her cheek. "Neasa, please? Come back to me. I can't live if you don't. I love you, darling. With all my heart." He bent to drop a kiss on her cheek, a finger flicking at the tears that she had wept. Looking around, Breck reached into his pocket, pulling out the ring that had been a grandmother's. He studied it before he reached to slip it on her finger, marking her as his, knowing that he would have to explain when she woke and awaken he was determined that she would.

Chapter 31

Patrick watched Breck closely before he approached, a chart in his hand as well as the medication bottle. Breck turned as he sensed someone there.

"Patrick?"

"Breck? I understand that this is your lady. Let's talk." Patrick set down the chart and bottle before he reached for his stethoscope and then assessed Neasa. "She's coming back from wherever it was that the seizure sent her. It was her first?"

"As far as I know. What caused it?"

Patrick lifted up the bottle. "These. This pain medication has a side effect that can sometimes cause seizures. But we had to run all the tests that we did. We'll repeat it before we discharge her in the morning. It seems that it was a combination of the medication and the stress that she was under. Her body just reacted adversely to both."

"She'll be okay?"

"Yes. I don't expect there to be any more seizures. It sometimes happens, Breck. We can't predict who or why." Patrick stayed for a few more moments, updating Breck as much as he could. "Buckley is here?" At Breck's nod, Patrick turned for the door. "I know he's not the pastor of your church, but I'll send him in. Your pastor is here as well."

"Buckley for now, I think. I'll speak to Daniel later."

Buckley paused as he stared at Patrick. "You're sure? Daniel's the pastor, not me."

"He asked for you. As a friend, I think, Buckley. Head on back."

Neasa roused in the morning, her headache better, but still feeling off. She stared around and sighed. The hospital again, she thought. When will I stay out of one? Neasa caught movement and found Breck sleeping beside her in an uncomfortable chair, moving restlessly. Her face softened as she studied him. I do love him, Lord, but I'm not sure I'm the right one for him. Feeling a weight on her finger, she frowned and stared at the ruby and diamond ring. I don't remember this. What did he do?

Breck watched Neasa through partially-opened eyelids, seeing when she found the ring and sighed to himself. He shouldn't have done that, he supposed, surprising her like that. It was not how it was to be. He was on his feet, reaching for her finger to withdraw the ring, startling Neasa, who stared up at him, fear briefly showing on her face.

"I'm sorry, darling. I shouldn't have done that. But I was afraid that they wouldn't let me stay."

Neasa stared at him and then the finger that she had curled towards her palm. "Taking it back, are you? Didn't mean it? I won't let you have it back, Breck. Not a chance."

"Neasa?"

"I mean it, Breck. You put it there, putting your heart out there for everyone to see. I see it. I have seen your heart for days." Neasa blinked back tears as she lifted her eyes to him. "Why?"

"Why? Why the ring? Because I love you dearly and deeply. I want to walk through life with you, to have you as the helpmeet that God chose for me. Only I don't know how you feel."

"How I feel? Right now, I feel like I have drummers in my head that are finally slowing down their beat. In my heart? I find that I love this tall handsome fellow, who has tried his best to protect me from everything, who wants me to walk through life with him. How can I not?" She pulled off the oxygen mask and tossed it aside. "I don't need this. Or maybe I do. Some fellow here in the room is taking away my breath."

"Neasa, darling? You mean that?"

"What? That I don't need the oxygen? Yes, I do. I also need out of here. Where are my clothes?" She smirked at the look on his face. "Breck? Sweetheart, I do. Now, find my nurse. And my discharge papers. If I don't have them, I'm still escaping. Only, didn't we do that once before?"

Breck had begun to grin as she spoke before he laughed quietly. "We did. Only this time, we're taking my truck and not your motorcycle. Although I still want to go on a long ride with a beautiful lady."

"And we will." Neasa watched as Breck looked around and then kissed her. Her eyes closed as he did so. "Stingy. Only one?"

Breck laughed again. "I can see how henpecked I'll be." He kissed her again before he reluctantly left to find her nurse, finding instead Patrick standing in the doorway, a huge smile on his face.

"Asked and answered? Congratulations, you two. I was just on my way in to see how Neasa was. Neasa, I think we need to keep you in for at least a week. You're too sick to go home." Patrick grinned at her squeal of outrage. "Seriously, though, you can leave. I know Doc will be checking on you, to say nothing of Brady and Cadee. Now, we need to note that you can't have that medication. And you need to lessen the stress in your life." He looked up as the couple laughed. "Not happening? Do your best. Here are your papers, young lady. Now, scoot. We need the bed for someone who is really sick."

Chapter 32

Branigan approached the whiteboards, writing down the information that he had discovered before he stepped back and then moved to the one that they had all decided would be Breck's logic problem. Burnie, the writer in the group, had set up one at one point and they had continued to use it. He added information to it, and then stood back. Something is missing, he thought. Something crucial. I'm just not sure what.

Benen stood beside him, Brennen on his other side, papers in their hands.

"What are we missing, fellows?" Branigan shot them both a look. "We are missing something."

"I know. I wish I knew what it was." Benen was frustrated. "How deep have we looked at that lawyer?"

"Not deep enough. Bradon was working on that, but he was called out on a search and rescue. He didn't know when he'd be back."

"Okay, so he's looking after that. What about the bones?" Benen was looking for anything that would move them ahead.

"Dallas is being very quiet on that. He hasn't said much." Branigan spoke up.

"No, and he can't. Not yet." Brady moved in to add to the board. "I'm looking at her father. I'm not liking what I find. He has a reputation for a temper and anger."

"We know that. What did you discover?" Brandon stood near them.

"That he has had charges laid and dropped. I have a source that has confirmed this. His wife was one of the ones who laid charges years ago, but dropped them."

"Domestic abuse?" Benen spun. "And then he tries this with Neasa? We need to talk to her mother."

"I have arranged that. Locklin and Buckley are heading that way tomorrow. She knows them and has agreed to speak with them. She sounded relieved that someone might finally believe her." Brady looked around. "I'm off. Fynn and I have a date tonight and I'm cutting it close as it is."

The remaining men watched him leave before they all looked at one another and then quietly put away their work and left, ready to pick it up on the morrow. Being married meant that they didn't spend hours and all night in the conference room. Not any more.

Neasa walked the room with Breck as he studied the walls, the marker he had handed her underlining certain names and events.

"How did they discover all this?" Her voice was barely a whisper.

"They all have sources they go to. Programs they run. They bounce ideas off of each other. Sometimes it is very quiet in here and at other times, very noisy. They joke with one another and laugh, but it is not at the person or persons. It is just a way to relieve their tension."

"I understand that, Breck. I need to be here, to talk with them." Neasa moved into his hug.

"I know. They'll be back in here as they can. I'll make sure that you're here."

"You have your own work to do, don't you? How are you managing without your secretary?"

"With great difficulty. We need to hire but at present, with what's going on with us? We have decided not to."

"Can I help in any way? I can at least answer the phone for you. And file. You do have filing that you do?"

"Darling, you are an answer to my prayer. Barnabas asked that, you know. He wanted to know if you might be interested." Breck kissed her and then led her from the room. They were meeting his parents for dinner and were running late.

"He did? I'll have to have a chat with him, I think. Putting ideas into your head. Signing me up for work without asking first." She smirked as he stared at her and then began to laugh.

"You just do that, darling. You just do that." He watched carefully as lights appeared in his rearview mirror, not sure anymore if they were friend or foe. He pulled into his parents' driveway and the car behind him flicked their emergency lights on and off. Breck breathed a sigh of relief.

Chapter 33

Breck listened closely as Buckley updated them all on his and Locklin's talk with Neasa's mother. It was not what he had expected. Looking at the men's faces, he could tell that they felt the same, other than for Blair. Blair caught his eye and nodded. He knew, didn't he, Lord? He knew that Dan wasn't Neasa's father, that he was her step-father. But where is her father?'

Buckley handed around pages of notes and documents.

"Her mother provided this for us. Her father disappeared when she was around two, Nevin one. His car was found in the lake, with evidence that led investigators to believe that he was in the car when it entered the lake. His body was never found."

Brody looked up, a look on his face that caught everyone's attention. "What if he wasn't? What if it was staged to look that way?"

"That's something that the original investigators were looking at. They didn't think that, in their conclusion. But we know that lake. Bodies can travel or be submerged and not be found."

Brody nodded. "Breck, did they ever say anything more about the bones?"

"No, they didn't." Breck stopped his pacing, his eyes on Brody. "Are you suggesting?"

"That it was her father? I am." Brody held up a paper. "This is from Emma. How she managed to get this, I don't know. It's the preliminary examination of the bones. Male. Early thirties. Caucasian. They found some bits and pieces of clothing. And a wedding band."

Breck sank into a chair, horror moving through him. "Her father?"

"They haven't concluded that yet, but I suspect that it is. Emma seemed to think so." Brody watched with compassion as Breck scrubbed at his face. "We can't say anything, Breck. Not until it's confirmed."

Nodding, Breck reached for the papers being handed him and read through them. He sat back, a puzzled look on his face. "I don't get why there. I really don't. The shelter has been there for so many years."

"Not that long. Neasa's what? Twenty-eight? The shelter building was run-down when the Foundation took it over twenty years ago. It's possible for someone to have been buried there and not found."

Brady looked up. "We need to talk to Barnabas and Bruce. Possibly Will. They might know more."

Breck looked up. "I can remember the shelter being dedicated. Twenty-five years ago. The land around it was not disturbed. It was left as it was, other than some landscaping around the building and the fence around the three sides. The work was not done near where we are planning the playground." He rose and suddenly left the room, needing to find some open space and fresh air. Lord, how do we do this? How do we tell Neasa that the man that she thinks is her father isn't? We need Your words and guidance on this.

Neasa watched as Breck paced, a frown on her face before she moved to stand in his way. His face lit up as he saw her and he reached to kiss her, holding her tight to him in almost a desperate manner.

"Breck? Are you okay?" She tilted her head back to look up at him.

"Not really. Just heard something disturbing. Walk with me."

The couple walked in silence for numerous circuits of the building before Neasa drew him down to a bench at the front of it.

"Breck? What is it?"

"Neasa, we had some disturbing news that we have to verify."

She looked disgruntled and distracted. "You too? I finally heard from Mom. Not what I wanted to hear. She told me that Dan is not my father, just my step-father. She apologized for that. When I asked her about my own father, she grew silent and just said that he was dead, that his body had never been recovered. She was calling Nevin after she spoke with me."

"That's all she said?" Breck watched Neasa closely.

"That's all. But she left out something. Something big and crucial. I could tell by how she hesitated and by the words that she was not saying." Neasa leaned against him. "I had this horrible dream or nightmare. That it was my father that we dug up. Do you know anything about it?"

"We just heard from Emma, darling. She had some information on your father. I was trying to clear my head before I spoke with you." His arm tightened around her. "Your father's car was found in Lake Erie, with the supposition that he was in it and was washed out. His body was not recovered in the lake."

"That's possible." She thought for a moment. "But there's more, isn't there?"

"There is. Emma pulled the preliminary medical report on the bones."

"My father?" Neasa looked up, horrified for a moment, and then she nodded. "That makes sick sense, you know. Dan was all jovial about doing the work, seemed to really want to, but there was a dark side to it that I saw. I don't think he really wanted to do it. Is he responsible?"

"That we don't know, Neasa. We don't have confirmation on the body as yet. They were still processing all the evidence." Breck grew silent, content just to sit and hold Neasa, bringing what comfort he could to her.

Chapter 34

Dallas watched Neasa closely later that afternoon before he sighed. *This is the part that I hate about this work, Lord, having to notify the next of kin. Her mother wasn't surprised. Nevin was angry and I can understand that. He was lied to all his life by the person who should have been honest with him. Now I have to speak with Neasa. Breck called me, Lord, just to warn me that Neasa has guessed. Please, Lord? I need the words from You that I just can't find myself.*

Neasa looked up from where she was standing in the rose garden, watching Dallas, and then walked towards him.

"Dallas? You have news?"

"I do, Neasa. Where's Breck?"

"He's on a conference call that will last the rest of the afternoon. Do you need him here?"

"I would prefer it, but let's head in. I don't like you out here right now." Dallas looked around, feeling someone watching them intently. "Someone is watching you, Neasa."

"I know they are. I have seen their shadows this afternoon, and also glimpses of them. They're bold."

Dallas stared at her before he spoke angrily. "Don't you care? Do you know what Breck would go through if something happened to you?"

Neasa stared back at him, no expression on her face. "I know exactly, Dallas. We have talked about that, many times. He knows I would not deliberately put myself out there, but I can't stop life. I have to live. I have to love. Even if it only for a short time. Don't you get that?" She brushed by him, heading for the building.

Dallas' head went back as his eyes closed. Lord, how do we reach her? She's reacting differently from the other ladies. And I really don't know how to get through to her about the danger that she is in. He found Neasa seated in a chair in the lobby, her eyes watching for him.

"Neasa?"

"Dallas? I know what you're going to say. That the bones we dug up were my father." She sighed, her eyes sliding closed, a single tear appearing on her cheek. She opened her eyes, anger briefly flickering in them. "Who?"

"That we don't know. And we are trying to determine that as best we can. It's been a lot of years, Neasa."

"I get that. I lived most of my life without knowing that Dan was not my father. Did he legally adopt us?"

"He did. I am sorry, Neasa, that I had to be the one to tell you." Dallas handed over the paperwork that he held in his hand. "This is what I can give you. I spoke with your mother earlier. She has no plans to return to this town. Were you aware of that?"

Neasa shrugged. "I gathered that much. She has always hated it."

"What can we do for you, Neasa?" Dallas wasn't quite sure how to proceed. Neasa was not like the other ladies from the building. Those ladies he had sort of known how to approach. Neasa was different.

"To tell you the truth, Dallas? I'm not sure." Neasa rubbed her hands along her jeans. "I thought that when I moved home, I would be happy and content to work for Dan. This has changed all that. Finding out that he was not my father? That has changed who I feel I am and makes my life seem like a lie. I mean, he would be kind to us at times, but stern. I always felt he was sterner with me than with Nevin. Maybe that's why I rebelled. He never wanted me to have the motorbike. I just went and got it. We had a fight over that. You know, Mom just stood back and never said a word. Nevin tried to intervene but Dan bluntly told him to stay out of it."

"I can see you rebelling." Dallas gave a grin. "You still are."

"I am?" Neasa stared at him and then past him before she nodded, a slow smile growing on her face. "I guess that I am. I need to stop though."

"Why? Breck loves you just as you are. He's a bit of a rebel at times."

"I know he is. He's looking at a motorcycle. Did you know that?" Neasa bit back a smirk, seeing Breck standing behind her, reflected in the window.

"He is, is he? And how does his future bride feel about that?" Dallas had a wide smile on his face.

"I think she feels it the right thing to do." Breck simply swept Neasa into his arms and sat down where she had been seated, grinning at her mock look of outrage.

"I can see you two, heading out on the open road. Just stay safe." Dallas sobered. "I was explaining to Neasa about our findings."

"It was her father?" At Dallas' nod, Breck sighed. "Do we know how?"

"No, unfortunately, there isn't a lot of evidence for that. We're looking into his medical history as well as his associates at the time."

Chapter 35

Breck watched his friends closely as they worked away before he looked down at the papers that he had just been shifting around. He didn't feel like working today, he thought, but I need to. These men need my attention to them, and that has been difficult. I need to get back to our weekly meetings and prayer time. He stood abruptly, a thought crossing his mind, and walked to the map that was tacked on the wall.

His finger tracing the area near the shelter, Breck paused at where the bones had been discovered and then moved his finger further away. A horrible thought came to him. What if that wasn't the only spot?

Brody had been watching him and exchanged a look with Brendon before he rose and approached him.

"Breck? You're thinking hard about something."

"I am, Brody. I had a horrible thought. That area was so abandoned and overrun with the Foundation took it over. What if Neasa's father wasn't the only one there?"

Brody nodded. "We had that same thought, Breck. I approached Dallas. They're planning on doing a search."

"They are? Good. Now, where do we stand with everything? And do you know what is strange? Neither Neasa nor I are receiving the nasty, horrible messages as she puts it. Not like you all did."

"You're not? That's weird." Bradon had approached. "I would have thought that you would be."

"No, not since that fellow was arrested in the city." Breck searched each of the men's faces, finding them all there.

"That is bizarre. No packages? No photos?"

Breck shook his head. "I mean, we can feel someone watching us. Neasa has glimpsed someone but not a good enough look to be able to describe whoever it was."

"Mind games, Breck. They're playing mind games with you. Trying to scare you without leaving any evidence. That's how they are doing it." Blair spoke from where he stood at the printer. "They'll up their game, now that it has come out about Neasa's father."

"It will." Breck leaned back against the wall, crossing his arms over his chest. "She's getting restless and is ready to revolt. I can't say as I blame her. She's never had this kind of restriction on her."

"Then, get out there. The weather is still nice enough that you could be out on her bike." Benen looked around as the door opened slowly and Neasa appeared, devastation on her face.

Breck shoved away from the wall and was to her before she could even speak, gathering her close, feeling the sobs that began to shake her body.

"Neasa? Darling? What is it?" He felt the phone that she had in her hand hitting him in the chest and reached for it, handing it to Branigan, who stared down at the photo and then at Neasa, shock and then anger on his face.

"My bike! He destroyed it! Why?" Neasa's voice was barely audible.

"What? What do you mean?" Breck looked up as her phone appeared in front of his face. He drew in a deep breath. "Your bike? Dan?"

"It has to be." She leaned back. "It is destroyed, in pieces, damaged beyond repair. Is he that angry at me?"

Breck had no words to comfort her. He could only hold her as tight as he could, his chin resting on her head, his eyes on his friends.

Anger flickered through the room before it turned to determination. The men shared a look and then dug back into their research, not willing to let Breck and his Neasa down. They all felt that there was someone behind Dan, someone driving him to do what he had. But who? Even Emma had been silent on that, and they all felt that was odd.

Breck pulled out a chair, seating Neasa, and then crouching down beside her. "You're sure it's yours?"

She nodded. "Look at the tank. There was an angel on it. It's there." She blinked rapidly, her tears turning to anger. "I want him, Breck. I don't want revenge. I just want to know why. What did I do to him that makes him that angry that he wants to destroy me? I don't have any riches. I have no trust funds or anything coming to me. Pops told me that." She paused, a thought crossing her mind. "What about Dad's people? Do we know anything about them?"

"We'll find out, darling. We'll find out. Right now, let's see what we can discover about Dan. Up for a challenge?" Breck grinned for a brief moment as she frowned at him and then nodded, determination on her face.

Chapter 36

Neasa looked around later that afternoon. She was still in the conference room, deep in reading the material that each of the men had handed her. She was surprised at how much that they had discovered, each finding something different. Neasa nodded. Of course, they would. They all think differently, now don't they?

Rising, she made her way to the kitchenette and stood, watching the kettle as it boiled before she made her hot chocolate. Grasping the cup in her cold hands, she wandered the perimeter of the room, her eyes assessing each one of the men. She was beginning to know the ladies, finding each one unique but all friends. She could see how they were pairing off. Sighing, Neasa wondered who it was that she would pair off with. Her mind turned to Barnabas and she began to pray for him. Lord, I feel that he is hurting, that someone hurt him in the past. I don't know who or how or why, but You do. Is his lady the one that I will be friends with? Lord, I need someone, a female, that I can be friends with, someone to laugh with, to share life. I know I have Breck, but us women need a friend,

She turned as she felt someone near her. Berneen stood her, reaching for her cup and handing her a fresh one, setting it down on a nearby table.

"You look thoughtful, Neasa." Berneen watched her closely.

"I am. It's been a bad day, all around." Neasa rubbed at her temple. "No, I don't have much of a headache. At least, not that kind." She looked up. "Dan destroyed my motorcycle. I found out that he's my step-father. Mom isn't speaking to me. And Nevin needs to be with Sarah. Breck is on conference calls, which I understand." She gave a small smile. "How does that sound?"

"Sounds like you need some girl time." Berneen swiped her mug and then deposited the cups into the sink, running water into them. She then linked an arm with Neasa, drawing her from the room, waving at the men as they looked up. "Don't worry. If Breck is looking for you, they'll send him my way. Come on. We need to start planning."

"Planning? On what?"

Berneen just shook her head, a finger to her mouth, as she walked Neasa to her apartment and then in.

"Sit. And reach for that pad of paper and pen. I picked up that habit from Breck. He always has a pad of paper and pen handy. Barnabas said he has always done that."

"Okay. Pen. Paper. Mug of chocolate, once more. Gingerbread cookies." She looked up, suspicion on her face. "Who told you that I like these cookies?"

Berneen began to laugh. "No one. I do, so I just assume everyone does. Now, you are going to be planning a wedding, aren't you?"

Neasa stared at her before she began to laugh. "Berneen! You know, I just asked the Lord for a friend, and you appear."

"I did, didn't I? I felt Him nudging me your way." Berneen sipped at her tea. "Now, what are you thinking?"

"I have no idea, to tell you the truth. Mom is refusing to speak with me. I sent her a text to let her know and she just responded "Oh?"." That hurts, you know. But I will go on with what I want. Sarah will help but she's not well right now. So I can't be burdening her."

Berneen nodded before she bent her head and prayed for Neasa and her family. Looking up, she found Neasa staring at her in surprise. "It's what we do, Neasa. We pray for one another as we need to. That's another thing your Breck is teaching us."

"He is? Teaching us to love one another as we should? I can see that." Neasa fiddled with the pen, tapping the end on the paper. "To tell you the truth? I never ever thought that I would marry. Right now, I'm afraid to. I'm afraid that I will bring more danger to Breck."

"And you will. We all did, both the fellows and the ladies. Baird was held captive for a few days where I was. The fellows came in, got us out, and then we were taken captive the very next day. I stepped in to marry him to save his life. He was beaten very badly. Buckley was with us and forced to perform the marriage. But I will say this. No matter what we went through, we love each other more and more each day.

God provided for us. He will provide for you and Breck. Now, do we plan a wedding or do we take on the fellows and try and solve this ourselves?"

"Solve it ourselves? Do you think we can?" Neasa looked up in surprise at that.

"I think we can take a stab at it. I have information that they haven't got yet. Emma, our friend, has been in touch. She sent me a whole lot of stuff. Darcie, another friend, has sent a profile of who she thinks is involved."

"Oh! Where is it?" Neasa watched as Berneen rose, heading for the office in the apartment and then sitting back down, handing over a pile of papers and keeping a stack for herself.

"Here. Read through it. I haven't yet, either. It just came, and that's when I went looking for you."

Chapter 37

Sitting back at last, Neasa looked over at Berneen, to find her watching her. Neasa grinned.

"How are we doing?" Berneen raised an eyebrow at her

"I think that we are getting somewhere. This bit about Dan? I didn't know that about him." Neasa poked at the paper she had been writing on. "He's related in some way to the man who had that restaurant. I would never have worked there, had I known that."

"That's interesting that he is. I wonder if the fellows have discovered that." Berneen sent off a text message to Baird and was surprised at his quick response. "No, they hadn't discovered that. And he wants to know how we did just that." Berneen began to laugh. "Give him ten minutes and he'll be up here."

"I say, five, and Breck will be with him."

The two ladies looked around as the door opened and both Baird and Breck appeared, as well as Dallas.

"We didn't include Dallas, did we?" Neasa grinned at Berneen.

"No, we didn't. Hmm. Should we tell them or should we wait?" Berneen looked up at Baird as he wrapped an arm around her.

"What have you ladies been up to?" Baird glanced at the clock. "It's supper time, ladies. I suggest that I fire up the grill, do some meat and veggies. We eat. We pray. And then we talk."

"Sounds like a plan." Berneen was on her feet, heading for the fridge. "I have chicken here and some burgers. I wasn't sure which we would want tonight, Baird."

Breck had been watching Neasa closely and knew that she would not make it through supper without speaking with him and Dallas. He drew her to her feet and then to the living room, beckoning Dallas to follow. He ducked his head to study her.

"Neasa?"

"Breck? Do you know what we discovered? That Dan is somehow related to the man I worked for?"

"He is?" Breck looked over at Dallas, to find him watching Neasa intently. "How did you discover that?"

"Emma sent it. We just found it out before you came in. There was a whole lot of information. And Darcie, I think it was, sent a profile. It fits Dan to some extent but not totally."

"Do you have that information that you can share, Neasa? Emma's been sending me information as well." Dallas looked down for a moment before he looked at Neasa, seeing how fragile she seemed at that moment.

"I guess." Neasa retrieved it from the kitchen. "Here. I want a copy of it."

———

"And you will have this one back. I just need to make some notes." Dallas scanned through it, taking photos of the pages that he needed to. "I'll investigate this, Neasa. Now, what else?"

"What else? Besides a destroyed dream?" Neasa blinked back tears. Her voice dropped to a mere whisper. "Do you know how long I had to work and save to buy my bike? And that dream is gone. Even if I were to get another one, it won't be the same."

"No, it won't, but you need to, maybe." Breck grinned as she shook her head at him.

"You're real definite there, you know?" Neasa turned back to Dallas. "What can you tell me?"

"Right now? We're working through everything that we have. I'm sorry I can't be giving out more information than that, but there is a lot of legwork and investigative work to do." Dallas grinned at her for a moment. "But right now? I think our supper is ready. Let's eat. And then we'll see where we stand."

Neasa looked disgruntled before she sighed. "I'm sorry. I know that it takes time. I just wish it was all over." She walked away from the two men, leaving Breck staring after her and Dallas watching Breck.

"Breck?"

Dallas' voice had Breck turning to him.

"Dallas? What didn't you say?"

"That you're the target now. I'm sure that Neasa has that figured out, but you both need to take extra precautions. We're still trying to determine who it is that put out the hit on you. And it is a hit, Breck. Someone wants you dead.”

Breck paled before his face grew grim. “We’ve been through this before, Dallas. Whoever it is will not win. God’s not finished with me here yet. Or at least, He hasn’t said that He is.”

Chapter 38

Hitting the rough pavement with his knees and then his hands, a deep groan came from Breck as he tried to recover from the brutal blow that he had just taken. His head hung down as he struggled to regain his breath. A savage blow from the ragged 2 x 4 sent him rolling towards a broken-down building and the open door. A shove from a booted foot had him tumbling down the broken concrete stairs to lie in a crumpled heap at the bottom, not moving. The door was slammed shut by his assailant, a bent rusty piece of pipe bracing it shut.

Dan stood in the shadows watching, a vengeful sneer on his face, before he reached into his pocket and pulled out a wad of bills, peeling a couple off and handing them to the young man who flung the 2 x 4 away from him. The young man grabbed the money and ran, not looking around at all. Dan's eyes followed him before they turned to the door. He strode away, a hateful laugh echoing behind him. As far as he was concerned, Breck was dead. He could now turn his attention to Neasa. If he couldn't get to her, then he would target Nevin. One of them would pay for his being arrested and placed in jail.

The late autumn darkness closed in, bringing shadows to the dimly lit area. Breck moved, groaning as he did so. He rolled to his side, pain shooting through him. He heard the faint rustlings of the critters in the basement of the building, the sound startling him, as did the feeling of critters crawling over him. His eyes slid closed and he was once more lost to consciousness. He didn't feel the trickle of blood that soaked into his hair or the cuts and scrapes that covered his face and hands.

A whisper of sound at the door and a slight scraping sound sent the critters scattering as the door squeaked open and a shadow appeared, that descended the steps. The man stooped over Breck before he glanced around. He raised Breck to his feet, struggling with Breck's height before he draped him over a shoulder and then staggered back up the stairs. He gently laid Breck down before he again closed the door, the pipe against it as he had found it. He raised the unconscious man to his shoulders once more and made his way as quickly as he could to the only shelter that he knew was safe, a rundown building blocks from where he had found Breck.

Breck was gently dropped to the rough pallet of ragged blankets that the man called his bed before the man turned to light the small fire that he always had ready. He rubbed his hands together before he turned back to Breck, carefully assessing the younger man. He sat back, before he reached for a bottle of water in his pack, opening it. Breck's head was raised enough so that he could swallow sips before he nodded, his eyes flickering open and closed.

"What do I do with you, Breck?" The man's whisper echoed through the room. "I need to get you to help, but I can't let anyone know that you're alive. He meant for you to die down there. And you would have. The door was the only way out and there is no chance that you could have opened it." He rummaged around in the room, finding the pot and carton of broth that he had stashed there, working to heat it and then spoon it into Breck, before he ate himself.

Early morning, with the dawn just breaking, the man roused, hearing footsteps ringing on the pavement outside. He was on his feet, to the door, his demeanour changing, his clear intelligent eyes taking on a mistiness as he ducked outside, to stand with his head lowered as the patrol officer approached.

"Davy? You're up and about early. Can't sleep?" The officer handed over the takeout cup of coffee and muffin that he had brought.

"Naw. I was asleep. You woke me with your heavy feet. Can't you walk any quieter?" Davy looked around, not seeing anyone else. "I need help, Joe."

"You do?" Joe kept his voice low as well.

"I do. I heard that a hit was put on on Breck."

"That's true. What would you know about that?" Joe watched the area around them, not looking directly at Davy.

"Cause I have him with me. He's hurt, Joe, hurt bad. I can't keep him awake. But I can't take him to the hospital. They'd find him."

"That they would. Let me think about this for a moment." Joe's voice raised. "Go on back to your bed, Davy. Enjoy your muffin. I'll bring another tomorrow for you."

"I'd be thanking you, Joe." Davy disappeared through the doorway, to stand in the dimness just inside it, watching Joe walk away. A breath of relief passed through him. Joe would make sure that Breck was taken care of. That he knew. He just had to keep him hidden until then, and that meant moving around in the daylight. That's where the danger was, he thought.

Dropping to his knees beside Breck, Davy shook his shoulder. "Wake up, Breck. We need to move."

Breck roused slightly, shaking his head. "No, I need to sleep, Dad. It's not a school day."

"No, it's not." Humour lashed through Davy's voice. "But we need to move, Breck. Come on, boy. Up with you."

Breck stood on unsteady feet, an arm wrapped around himself as the pain intensified. His face was white under the scrapes, cuts, and bruises. Davy gathered his things, stuffing them into his pack, and then shoved a shoulder under Breck's arm, knowing the younger man just didn't have the ability to stand and walk, not on his own.

"We're moving, Breck. I need to keep us on the move for the day. I have help coming but I just don't know when. And I just don't know how bad you're hurt."

Chapter 39

Davy watched Breck closely over the day, as they moved from bench to bench, ending up in another abandoned building. It was one that Davy used a lot, and he knew that Joe would find him. That's what Joe did.

Breck sank down to the cold, earthen floor, not even feeling the dampness or chill that met his body. He didn't care. All he knew was that he hurt and hurt badly all over and that this man he was with had kept him on the move all day, despite his protests that he just couldn't do it. He didn't see Davy setting up a fire or finding ragged blankets that he had stuffed into a crevice, spreading them out of the floor and then rolling Breck onto them, covering him with another one.

His head turning as he heard a noise, Davy moved towards the doorway, extinguishing his fire on the way. His hand went up to shield his eyes as a bright light flashed at him before it moved around the room. A gentle hand took him to one side and Joe's voice whispered in his ear.

"I had trouble finding you, Davy. You moved a lot today."

"I had to, Joe. I had to for Breck's sake. I saw men looking for someone."

"I know, Davy. I know. Here, let's get you out of here. Where's your stuff?"

"Here." Another man handed Davy his knapsack. "We've got him, Davy. We'll look after him. You need to come with us."

"I can't, Joe. I can't." Davy disappeared before either man could stop him, leaving them staring at one another.

"It's what he does, Ed. He helps and then disappears."

"So I am told." Ed turned to the other two men with him. "Where to, fellows?"

"I would say the building, Ed. If we can come up with some excuse to get him there." Joe looked around. "How close to the door are you parked?"

"Not close enough to. I'll move in near the back door. It's easier to get at." Ed was gone and then they heard the quiet sound of the vehicle as it stopped outside the door.

The three men in the building quickly moved Breck to the vehicle before Ed drove away as quickly as he could, the four men searching the darkness for anyone watching. Joe saw Davy briefly appear, a hand raised to acknowledge him before he once more disappeared into the darkness.

"They'll be watching the building for Neasa." Ed shot a look back at Breck, slumped in the middle of the back seat, his eyes closed.

"They will be." Joe had his phone out. "Let me call Barnabas. We can likely go into the loading dock that they have there. Barnabas? Joe Barrett. I'm good. And you? Breck? We heard that there was a hit out on him. Listen. I have a friend with me. Can we come in through the loading dock?"

Barnabas stared at the phone he had pulled from his ear before he was speaking. "Joe? The loading dock? Sure. I'll meet you there. We've upped the security around here. Branigan will meet you by the gate and lead you in."

"Sounds good. Fifteen minutes, I think, Ed says." He tucked away his phone, his own eyes on Breck. "Branigan will meet us, Ed."

"Sure. I thought there would be someone there."

Branigan watched carefully as Ed drove into the loading dock before he ducked in, the overhead door closing behind him. He approached Barnabas, who stood waiting for the men to exit the vehicle, a frown on his face when they didn't, only Joe slipping quickly out and closing the door behind him.

"Joe? Why the mystery?" Barnabas stared at the officer that he knew well.

"We have Breck, Barnabas."

"Breck? You have him." Barnabas moved to go around Joe, stopping as Joe held up his hand. "What's wrong?"

"He was beaten badly, sometime yesterday, and shoved down some cement stairs. A fellow on the street found him, took care of him overnight, and then kept him on the move today. We don't want to take him into the hospital, not unless Doc or Brady says we should. Is either one around?"

"Both are." Barnabas turned as he heard Branigan running from the area. "Branigan will get them. Do we need the stretcher?"

"I would say yes, but we need to get him out of here and then have us leave. It's too obvious that we have something or someone for you, driving in as we did."

"True." Barnabas watched as Breck was carefully maneuvered from the back seat, and arms over the shoulders of two of the men, walked to the infirmary, Brady appearing as they reached the door. "Brady?"

"Got it, Barnabas. Doc's on his way, Branigan said. So is Anna. Beck and Bonnie are with Neasa."

"I know. Get him in there, and I'll head up. Joe, Ed. Thanks."

Joe and Ed simply waved, following the other two officers back to their vehicle, waiting for security to open the door and let them out. Joe stared back at the building, knowing that Breck was in good hands, but worried about Davy.

"Davy? How much trouble is he in?" Ed's voice reached through the dim lighting in the vehicle.

"A lot, I would say. But he can take care of himself, much better than anyone would think." Joe didn't let on that Davy was an undercover officer, had been for a number of years, and was due to come back into the office, taking up a position on the detective squad.

Chapter 40

The previous afternoon, Neasa had gone looking for Breck, just needing to see him and feel his arms around her. When knocking at his door brought no answer, she headed for the main floor and his office. She knocked and then finally opened the door, finding the lights off and no Breck. She paused, a hand rubbing at her forehead, a tiny headache beginning behind her eyes. She was frustrated with those, she thought.

Heading for the conference room, she opened the door and then entered, watching as Brandon, Bradon, and Burnie were at work, looking up to greet her.

"Have you seen Breck?"

The three men looked at one another before shaking their heads.

"I think he was heading into town this morning. He said something about having to go to city hall with some paperwork." Burnie rose and approached her. "He's not back?"

"No, he's not. I can't find him." Neasa was worried and it showed.

"Neasa? What's up?" Bradon had approached as had Brandon.

"Dallas was out yesterday. He said that there's a hit, as he called it, out on Breck. Breck was trying not to let me know." Neasa wrapped her arms around herself. "And now I can't find him."

"Listen, I'll head into town." Bradon was moving towards the door. "Ennis will come with me." He didn't let on, but her words had hit home with him. Breck was the latest of them to have had a hit put out on him.

"I'll check out the gym and that area." Brandon moved away as well, leaving Burnie to reach out a hand and direct Neasa to a nearby chair.

"Neasa? Did he talk to you today at all?"

"He did. About mid-morning. Just to say he loved me and that he would be back this afternoon." Neasa rose and paced the room. "This is not the Breck I know. To say that and not do it."

"No, it's not Breck. Let me call Dallas and let him know."

Neasa shook her head. "He's in court, he said. We can't disturb him." She spun, walking along the whiteboards, studying the new information. "You fellows have been busy."

"We have been, Neasa. We were to meet with you and Breck tomorrow morning. He requested that. There is some information that we're still confirming."

"I see. What's this?" Neasa pointed to a name. "Who is this?"

"That lady? We're still confirming it, but we believe that she is your natural mother. And Nevin's." Burnie watched as she spun, shock on her face. "The woman that you knew as your mother? She is actually your step-mother. What we have determined is that your mother died from cancer about two months after

Nevin was born. Your father remarried quickly, not able to make it work raising you two."

"And then he died about ten months later? Burnie? This sounds like one of your books."

Burnie grinned. "It does? That what they told me about Muir and me." He sobered. "I'm sorry, Neasa. Breck wanted to be here when you were told."

"And he's not. What else has been false about my life? My grandparents?"

"The ones that you see? They are your father's. They were adamant that they not be kept out of your life. The woman that you know as your mother is not with them. She hasn't been."

"I see. That makes sense then that I hadn't heard any other voices. I haven't had a chance to call Pops or Grams yet, with what all has been going on. And that's not me." Neasa sat, her arm leaning on the table. "I need to."

"You do, but I would wait for the moment. Right now? We need to figure out where your fellow is." He pulled out his phone. "It's Bradon. Bradon? His truck? Oh. No sign of him? Okay. Ennis will? Sure. Call it in. I'm still in the conference room with Neasa. They are? That's good."

Burnie put away his phone, his eyes on Neasa. "Bradon found Breck's truck, but it was in the downtown area."

"Downtown? That's strange."

"It is. He sometimes heads that way when he's in town, just to check on the people there, to make sure that they don't need anything. That's what he was likely doing. Bradon will call it in."

"Oh. Okay. His parents?"

"They were on their way here. Apparently, Breck had asked them for dinner."

"He did? I didn't know that." Neasa was on her feet, heading for the lobby, not seeing Burnie reaching to stop her.

Burnie watched her move away, shaking his head. Lord, she's hurting in so many ways. Now, Breck is gone, and she has to feel like she's sinking or lost at sea or something. Help us to find him and find him quickly.

Chapter 41

Bonnie watched as Neasa paced her apartment the next afternoon. They had stayed with her, not willing to leave her on her own. Beck had headed for Barnabas, to see what he could discover. There had been no word as yet, and both of Breck's parents were worried.

"Neasa?" Bonnie watched as Neasa turned towards her. "What can I do for you?"

Neasa sighed before she sat beside the older lady on the couch. "I'm not sure. I'm just so confused right now. I don't know where to even start."

"Just start talking. We'll figure it out as we go along." Bonnie reached to wrap an arm around the younger woman, bowing her head to pray for her.

"Thank you, Bonnie." Neasa wiped at her eyes. "I had some really bad news yesterday. Breck knew and had wanted to tell me." She looked up at the ceiling, blinking as she did so, her hands twisting on her lap. "The woman I thought was our mother? Isn't. She's a step-mother. Our real mother died when Nevin was two months. Then Dad was killed when about ten months later. It's just so confusing. I'm not even sure if the last name I have is the correct one."

"Let them sort it out for you, Neasa. Right now, you're needing to heal. I would like to step in as your mother, if I may. Not to replace her, but to be there for you." Bonnie watched as Neasa struggled with her emotions.

"Thank you, Bonnie. Can I call you Mom?" Neasa turned to her, hope on her face.

"You can, my dear. You can. Call Beck Dad, if you want. You'll be our daughter. I always wanted one, but God didn't send us one."

Finally stretching out and sleeping, Neasa didn't hear Beck return or Bonnie moving around her apartment. She didn't rouse as the older couple ate their meal, leaving hers in the fridge for when she awoke.

Barnabas tapped at the door late that evening, finding Beck opening it.

"Barnabas? I didn't expect to see you tonight." Beck studied the younger man. "Have you word?"

"Where's Neasa? Is she still up?"

Beck pointed to the living room. "She's asleep in there. Go on in, son." Bonnie stood with her hand on Beck's back, watching as Barnabas crouched down beside the couch.

A hand on Neasa's arm, Barnabas spoke quietly.

"Neasa, can you wake up for me?" He grinned as she frowned at him before she pushed her hair away from her face.

"Barnabas? I was sleeping. This had better be good."

"Oh, I know that you'll think so. Breck is here." He waited, opening his mouth to speak again as Neasa sat up abruptly.

"Breck? Where?"

"The infirmary." Barnabas moved quickly out of the way as Neasa shot to her feet, running for the door without a thought for her shoes. The door almost slammed behind her, she had opened it with that great of force.

"Breck?" Bonnie moved forward.

"He's in the infirmary, Beck, Bonnie. He has been hurt." Barnabas stared at the door. "I'm glad that I wasn't standing in her way."

Beck began to laugh. "I think she would have just run you down. Where are her shoes, love?"

"Right here?" Bonnie held up the shoes that she had retrieved. "And I have her keys. Let's go find our son."

Neasa didn't see the men waiting in the hallway, their ladies with them, or even see Hailey and Hollie as they huddled together near the door. All eyes were on her as she ran past them, heading for the infirmary, through the door, and beside Breck before anyone could even reach out a hand to stop her.

Doc looked up and nodded towards her, Cadee turning and approaching her.

"Neasa? We need you to step back for a moment." Cadee's arm around her drew her away, even as Neasa struggled to get back. Barnabas was there as well, his arm around her, Cadee nodding at him before she returned to help Doc. Brady watched from the other side of the stretcher.

Barnabas turned her towards the door, not letting her return to Breck, even as she continued to try that.

"We'll wait right outside here, Neasa. They won't be long, they said."

Neasa stared at the closing door. "I need to be with him, Barnabas."

"And you will. Right now, Doc needs this time. He's been beaten, Neasa."

"Beaten? Is that why?" Neasa stared wildly around before she ran, not hearing the cries for her to stop and to wait. She hit the door in the lobby, running through it to the outside, the darkness covering her path. Where could she go, she wondered? Where? It's my fault that he's hurt. She continued to run, finally stopping in the rose garden, dropping to her knees beside a bench, heart-rending sobs rising from her.

Blair stood and watched, before he moved forward, reaching to gather her up, surprised that she didn't fight him. He looked around, sensing someone there.

"Who's there?"

"Just me. Davy. I just wanted to know how Breck it."

"Davy? You found him? Come. Come with me."

Davy hesitated and then moved forward, following Blair, keeping in the shadows as much as he could. He stopped as he stepped in the lobby before he

moved towards the infirmary. Then he turned and left.
He couldn't and shouldn't be here, he thought.

Chapter 42

An hour later, Neasa stood with Breck's hand tight in hers, her other hand on his face. The stubble on his cheek was rough under it, but she didn't care. He was here, even though he had not awakened as yet. Doc wasn't overly concerned, he told her. If Breck didn't awaken soon, then they would need to transport him to the hospital. At the moment, none of them wanted that.

Neasa prayed hard, prayed for her fellow to awaken, for the ones responsible to be caught and brought to justice. She really had no idea how to pray. She turned her head as she heard soft footsteps.

"Hailey. Hollie. Should you be here?"

The twins nodded.

"We need to be with you, Neasa. He's like our big brother." Hollie whispered even as she leant against Neasa. "Is he okay?"

"Doc said he was beaten. We were told that he was likely shoved down some steps. What else happened, we're not sure." Neasa looked at Hailey. "Hailey?"

"It's okay, Neasa. We can go now. We just needed to make sure."

Neasa reached to hug the two girls. "Come back in the morning. He may be awake then." She watched them walk away before she reached to wrap a blanket around herself and then picked up the mug of hot chocolate Benen had brought her, waving away her thanks.

Barnabas raised his head after Buckley had finished his prayer. The men had all gathered in the conference room, grim looks on their faces, before they bowed for prayer. It was time, he knew, that they pulled back from their work, as they had so many times already, and worked towards finding the ones responsible for Breck's beating, to solve the mystery surrounding Neasa. And it was becoming more and more of a mystery. Just who she was? That was what was puzzling all of them.

"Barnabas?" Brennen looked around at his friends. "Do we know what happened?"

"Joe brought him out." The men recognized the name of an officer that they knew from church. "He was beaten sometime yesterday. Dumped down some stairs. A homeless man found him and took care of him. Joe said he moved Breck all over the downtown today, trying to protect him."

Benen spoke up. "An undercover officer, I have no doubt."

Brody stared at him. "I never thought of that. But likely. But where do we go from here?"

"I talked to Neasa. She's aware of what we found. Now, how far along on that are we?"

"Not where we need to be. I'm finding out all sorts of stuff about the step-mother. She had reported Dan for abuse but always backed away from it when questioned. That was in the early years. She has finally talked to me." Branigan looked up. "I pulled the legal stuff with her. Told her I was a paralegal and if she wanted help, I would see that she could get it. She's refused, for now, just glad she said that Neasa and Nevin were away from Dan."

"Only they're not. Barnabas, where is Nevin and his Sarah right now?" Brendon looked up from his notes.

"They're with friends. Not our friends, but their friends. And away from here."

"That's good. He'll go after Nevin if he can't get to Neasa. I hope he doesn't know who the friends are."

"Nevin said that he won't." Barnabas looked up as the door opened and Dallas appeared.

"Dallas? I thought you had to be ready for court in the morning."

"I was but the case was postponed. Will told me to get myself out here and stay until we solved this. He put in a leave of absence for me, letting me do that, but keeping access to all my sites and programs." Dallas sat slowly, a thank you to Brandon for the mug of coffee set in front of him. "What's going on? Will just told me to talk to you."

Barnabas nodded. He had called his father and Bruce had contacted Will.

"We have Breck."

Dallas choked on his coffee. "I'm sorry. I thought that you said you have Breck."

"We do. Someone took care of him and then some of your officers brought him out here tonight. So far, Doc thinks that between himself, Brady and Cadee, they can manage to treat him."

"How bad?" Dallas' face grew stern.

"Bad enough that he hasn't roused yet. He was beaten, Doc thinks with a 2 x 4. We think he was shoved down some stairs and then locked into a building. Whoever it was that found him took him from there and then moved him around all day. It didn't help him any physically, but it likely saved his life."

"I see." Dallas reached for a pen and paper. "If he was locked into a building, that had to be in the downtown area. And some of those buildings? You put a board or something against a door and that would block the only way out. There are no windows in some of them."

"That's our guess." Baird spoke up. "I would like to thank whoever it was."

"We all do." Dallas rose and walked towards the whiteboards, silent as he studied them. "You fellows have found a lot of information. I haven't had the time to devote to it as I should. Being one short on the detective team means a lot of overtime."

"We get that, Dallas. Emma's been sending us information. She sent Neasa a profile, she said."

"That she did. I have it. I'll gladly share if Neasa says I can. I can't put a name to the person described but he or she sounds so familiar."

"He or she?" Bradon spoke up. "You're thinking female?"

"We always do, Bradon. Now, how late do we work? And Barnabas, I'm told there is an apartment here that I am to use for the next few days."

Chapter 43

Rousing early in the morning, Breck stared around the room, recognizing it as the infirmary at home. He sighed. Someone had brought him home, but who? He turned his head, feeling a hand touching his face, and frowned.

"Do I know you?" He stared at the young woman standing beside his bed, the paleness of her face and the dark shadows under her eyes showing her fatigue.

"Do you know me?" Neasa stared at him before she repeated herself. "Do you know me?" Her hand went up. "This is your ring on my finger, buster. We're engaged. How dare you ask me if you know me!" She swatted his arm, not seeing the wince that he gave.

"We are? I'm sorry. Everything is foggy right now."

"Foggy? Is that your excuse? Breck! How dare you forget me!" The tears that she could not contain sparkled on her cheeks as she backed away. Standing with her back to the door, Neasa faced him down.

"I'm sorry. We're engaged?" Breck lowered the bed rail and swung his feet off the bed, sitting for a moment to let his head clear. He stared down at his clothes, wondering how they got so dirty, and why he was so sore. He slid off the bed, wincing once more as the slight jar that went through his body started the pain before he moved towards Neasa. He stood, a hand flat against the door on either side of her head, and studied her.

"We are. You told me that you loved me. How could you forget? I don't need someone to forget." Neasa swiped at the tears, jumping as Breck's hand cupped her cheek.

"I'm sorry. My mind is foggy. No one should forget as beautiful a lady as you are." He stared down at her and without even thinking bent to kiss her.

Neasa shoved at him, sending him toppling backward to the floor. Horrified, she stood, hands over her mouth before she was on her knees, helping him to sit up.

"I'm sorry. I shouldn't have done that."

"It's okay. I shouldn't have kissed you."

Neasa smacked his arm once more. "Of course you should. We are engaged. And I am not letting you go. So take that, buster." She looked around as the door opened, and Doc peeked in cautiously, having heard her raised voice.

"Breck? You're up, I think. Neasa? Any reason you two are sitting on the floor?"

"Don't ask, Doc. Talk some sense into this man. He's forgotten that we're engaged. He doesn't remember me, he tells me, and then he has the nerve to kiss me." Neasa was on her feet, running from the room, not hearing Guenivere as she called for her.

"Breck? Did you really do that?" Doc helped Breck to his feet and back to the bed.

Breck stared at the door, waiting for Neasa to return. "I did, Doc. I guess that I shouldn't have."

Doc shrugged. "You two are engaged, but I don't think it was a good idea. Your kissing her, that is."

Breck suddenly grinned. "She's a firebrand, isn't she?"

Doc began to laugh. "That she is, son. That she is. She's just what you need. She doesn't back down from you, not like the other ladies do when you go all stern and dark."

"No? That's unusual." Breck sat, bemused. "I'm really engaged?"

"You are, Breck. She's going through some pretty bad stuff right now, which is why you were beaten up and dumped. Someone found you and then Joe and some fellow officers brought you home."

"I don't remember much after going to city hall." Breck slid from the bed, standing for a moment to catch his balance. "I need to go change and then find my lady. What's her name?"

Doc stared at him and then began to laugh heartily. "Don't tell her that you can't remember her name. She'll hit you again. It's Neasa."

"Neasa? A beautiful name for a beautiful lady." Breck walked slowly away, leaving Doc shaking his head after him.

Showered, shaved and in clean clothes, Breck practically inhaled the coffee that he had made before he turned to the door, opening it and then closing it behind him. He stopped. He needed to find Neasa, only where would she be? He stared at the doors on his floor before he shook his head. Right now, he had no idea which apartment she would be in if she was even in one of them. He turned as he heard Devaney's voice behind him.

"She's in the apartment next to you, Breck. You have that lost look on your face." She grinned at him.

"I do, don't I? I'm in the dog house and not sure how to get out of it."

"Grovelling is good. Lots of grovelling. Flowers are also right up there." She continued to grin. "Only I don't think you're in any shape to go out and buy her flowers."

"No, I'm not. That will have to wait. Thanks, Devaney." He turned to the apartment door, tapping at it, hearing Neasa's voice telling whoever it was to go away.

"Neasa? Please? Open the door."

Neasa flung the door open, standing with her hands on her hips, staring at him in disbelief.

"How dare you come around me? You don't remember me. Go away!"

Breck simply shook his head. "Please, Neasa? Can we at least talk?"

Neasa stared at him, before she shoved by him, slamming the door behind her, and then heading for the lobby. He reached to stop her, finding her stiffen at his touch. Lord, how do I do this? I've hurt her, without meaning to. Please, Lord? What do I do?"

Neasa stood, her back straight as she faced away from him. "Breck? What is it exactly that you want to say?"

"That I'm sorry. I know that's my ring on your finger. I recognize it. I just don't remember all that well. My mind's confused."

She snorted. "Your mind's confused? That's a mouthful, Breck." She turned, eyeing him. "And what else?"

"I'm grovelling here, Neasa. I was told to grovel to get out of the dog house. Oh, yes. And flowers. Only I was told I wasn't in any shape to go and buy you any."

Neasa looked past him, seeing Devaney standing there, a grin on her face. "Oh, I see. Grovelling, are we? How much grovelling are you prepared to do?"

Breck stared at her before his eyes narrowed, catching the smirk that she was trying to hide.

"I don't know about that now. Grovelling seems kind of low." He simply swept her into a hug, finding her struggling at first before she hugged him back. "Work with me, please, Neasa? I want to remember. I truly do."

Chapter 44

Opening the door to the conference room, Breck waited while Neasa entered before he followed her and stood beside her, his narrowed eyes taking in the activity. Everyone is here, aren't they, Lord? That means we must be making progress. Only I have no idea and I need to know. Heal me, please, dear Lord. And protect the lady that they say is mine.

Dallas stood from where he had been sitting, approaching them, seeing not a couple but two people. He frowned as he felt the tension between them before Neasa moved away, to stand staring at the whiteboards before she turned to speak with Bradon.

"Breck?" Dallas was hesitant to even question him.

"Dallas? You're here."

"I am. Will sent me to work on this with you all. How are you?"

"Not great. I hurt all over. I don't remember what happened." Breck paused, sadness on his face. "And I don't really remember Neasa."

"You don't remember her? You're engaged. How could you not?" Dallas simply shook his head, a hand on Breck's arm steering him to a chair.

"I don't know. She didn't take it well."

"And do you blame her? Do you remember anything of what's going on with her?"

Breck shook his head. "It's like I have a huge gap there, that I can't remember things. I see flashes and bits and pieces."

"Okay." Dallas looked around, beckoning to Buckley. "First, let Buckley pray for you, and then we'll work with you to get you to where you need to be. Neasa has been in and out for the last few days, helping in any way that she can. Just thought that you should know that."

"Thanks, Dallas. I do." Breck watched as Neasa moved from work station to work station, speaking with each of the men. He frowned. "Buckley? What's she up to?"

"Neasa? You don't know? She'll come in and speak with each one of us. Not about what's going on with her. Just to see how we are, what she can pray for, how the ladies are, how the littles ones that are here are. She has a gift, Breck, that I don't see very often. A gift to reach down and find out what she wants to know about a person so that she can better understand them and then pray for them. She's like you in that."

"Yeah, about that." Breck sighed, his eyes on his friend. "I can't really remember her. She didn't take it well."

"Do you blame her? Let me pray for you, Breck. You're like Neasa. You just give and give, without asking for anything in return. It's our time to return that to you."

Breck finally looked once more, to find Neasa had seated herself beside him, her hand on his. He shared a look with Buckley before he turned to her.

"Neasa?"

"Breck? Where do we go? Sorry, Buckley. I shouldn't have asked in front of you."

"It's okay, Neasa. I can play the pastor role again if you like." He simply grinned at her. "Or I can get up and walk away."

"Stay, I think, Buckley. We may need a referee." She smirked as Buckley began to laugh, Breck staring at her in disbelief. "Yes, a referee. Breck, you tell me that you don't remember me or what we've been going through. You are about to get a crash course in it. The men all tell me that you have worked tirelessly to solve the adventures that they went through. Now, it's their turn to give back. They have amassed an amazing amount of information. Dallas was sent out here by Will to aid in the investigation and do what he does best. Make it legal." She pointed to the papers in front of her. "This is a summation that Burnie has prepared. It's good. He's treated it like a plotline for one of his mystery stories."

"He does that. It's the author in him, how he thinks." Breck reached for the papers. "May I?"

"You may. Before we start, Buckley, please pray. I sense that we are coming into a very dangerous part of our lives. Almost losing Breck to that building? I can't handle it if that really happens. He is my lifeline to reality right now, even though he says he doesn't remember me."

Breck read through the sheaf of papers, stopping as he had barely started to reach for a pen and the pad of paper Buckley had set down. He finally sat back, staring across the room, before he turned to Neasa, finding her asleep, her head down on her folded arms. Someone had found a blanket and tucked it around her. He laid his hand gently on her hair, fingering a strand, before he stood, heading for the coffee pot and refilling his mug, before he turned, watching the activity. About half of the men had left, having other commitments that they needed to get to. Breck turned to the whiteboards, moving past them slowly, reading each one, finally reaching for a pen and heading for a blank one, jotting down a concise summary of what he had just read.

Barnabas approached him, his head tilting to watch his friend.

"Breck?"

Breck nodded. "If you heard that I don't remember Neasa at the moment, it's true. And she has told me off about that." He sighed, his eyes rising to the ceiling. "How do I do this, Barnabas?"

"By doing what you are doing. Helping to solve this. Praying. Just being with her. Doc would tell you that you did this to protect someone, possibly yourself. I would say that you did this to protect Neasa, or else the person involved in one that you didn't expect and that shock has done this to you."

"That may be." Breck turned to watch Neasa sleeping. "She's wearing out, my friend. How do we solve this and soon?"

Barnabas sighed. "That we are working on. We need some more information." His voice halted as he watched Breck's face. "What did you remember?"

"Dan was there. He was off in the shadows. I saw him and slowed my steps, not wanting to approach him. That's when someone hit me." Breck looked at Barnabas. "I have no idea who that was, but Dan was there. He watched without stepping in to stop it."

"Then, he's likely the one who arranged it." Dallas had approached the two men. "Let me call that in, Breck. I know we need to get your statement and I'll have someone come out. Don't say anything more."

Chapter 45

Neasa awoke, stretching as she did, her eyes on Breck as he stood talking with Barnabas and Dallas. *Will he remember me, Lord? Or I am to walk away from the one I love so much? I can't do this, Lord, and I don't understand why You are asking me to. I know You are in control. Guide our steps. Put a watch on our mouths.* She reached into a pocket for her phone, searching the messages. She breathed a sigh of relief. None from an unknown number. She smiled at Nevin's message. Neasa missed her brother but understood why they had to stay apart. She was just too dangerous for him and Sarah to be around.

Rising and heading to make herself a hot chocolate, Neasa hesitated, a thought crossing her mind. She turned instead and headed for the board holding the logic problem, her finger tracing some names before she crossed out one and added another, changing the perspective of the mystery. *Why that name?* Neasa had no idea why.

Brandon had been watching Neasa and rose to move to stand beside her, reading what she had done.

"Her? Why?"

Neasa shrugged. "I have no idea. I can remember her being around Dan's shop and them being in deep discussion, changing the subject if Nevin or I approached. She wasn't a landscaper. Far from it. She refused to get her hands dirty. With dirt, that is. I often wondered if she was involved in a crime."

Benen stood beside them, staring at the board and then down at the paper he held.

"How'd you do that?" He was stunned.

"Do what?" Brandon peered around Neasa at him.

"Find her. I just did."

Neasa shook her head. "I don't know. I just remembered her. Why?"

"Because she was just arrested for something else. Dallas is looking for you. He was out in the lobby." Benen turned as the door opened and Dallas entered, searching for Neasa.

Dallas paused beside Breck, studying the other man closely. He could see the pain that Breck was still in and the fatigue that was weighing him down.

"Breck, go home. Go to bed for a while. You're out on your feet."

Breck nodded, scrubbing his hands down his face. "I know, Dallas, but I don't want to leave Neasa."

"She'll be here when you come back. Go on. I'll tell her." He watched at Breck reluctantly nodded and then moved away.

Neasa turned as she heard Dallas' voice behind her.

"Dallas?"

"Neasa. I sent Breck off to get some sleep. He wasn't ready to leave you. He needs this rest, Neasa."

"I know that he does. But I don't know where I stand with him. Not anymore." Neasa moved quickly away from the three men, heading out of the door, to stand in the lobby before she ran for her own apartment, locking the door behind her. She threw herself onto her bed as deep sobs shook her body. The sobs weren't just because of Breck. Neasa had reached her breaking point. She wept for the father and mother that she could not remember. For Nevin. For Sarah. For the lostness that she now found herself in. She finally slept, sobs still shaking her body. They would be healing but she still faced danger.

Three hours later, Bonnie stared at her son before she looked at Beck, who also stood staring at Breck.

"What do you mean, son? You don't remember Neasa?" Bonnie finally asked the question.

"That. I remember the ring, but not on her finger." Breck sighed, running his hand through his rumpled hair. "I made the mistake of asking if I knew her."

Bonnie began to laugh, picturing that very event. "Went well, did it? How much did she tell you off?"

"Mom!" Breck finally nodded. "She did just that, Mom. And then shoved me away from her."

"Can't say as I blame her, son." Beck moved past Breck towards the kitchen. "It must have been a shock for her. She hadn't slept much when you were away."

"She hadn't? I didn't know that." Breck took the mug of coffee offered to him.

"No, you wouldn't. She's hurting, Breck, from what she has found out about her past. To be going through this and then have you disappear? It shook her world in a way that I can't even begin to understand." Beck slid back a chair and sat, his mug hitting the table as he watched his son.

Bonnie moved away, heading for the apartment next door, and the young lady that she had taken to her heart. Not getting an answer, she sighed and reluctantly reached for the key that Neasa had given her. She entered the apartment, searching for Neasa, standing beside her bed, seeing the traces of the tears that had been shed. Bonnie reached for a blanket, covering Neasa, and then headed for the bathroom, returning with a warm damp cloth that she used to wash away the tear tracks.

Bonnie settled into the living room, not willing to let Neasa stay on her own. Her head bowed as she prayed for her daughter, as she had begun to think of Neasa. No in-law about it, she had decided.

Neasa roused in the late afternoon, finding the bedside lamp on, and not remembering turning it on. She felt the blanket covering her and frowned before she rose, showered, and changed to fresh clothing. Heading for the kitchen, she paused as she saw lights on and grew fearful, tiptoeing forward until she spied Bonnie in the kitchen.

"Bonnie?"

Bonnie spun before she moved to wrap Neasa in a hug. "Neasa? You've slept. You needed that, child. Now, I have some soup ready for you. I hope that was okay."

Neasa shrugged. "I don't have much of an appetite."

"I didn't think that you would. Too much going on. Here. Sit. We'll eat, pray, and then decide what to do with that thick-headed young man next door."

Neasa stared at her. "Bonnie?"

"He told us, Neasa, that he couldn't remember you and that you told him off." Bonnie began to laugh, bringing a smile to Neasa's face. "I would have loved to see that. Not many people get a chance to do that."

"Devaney told him that he needed to grovel and grovel a lot. And that he needed to bring me flowers."

"So that's why." Bonnie nodded. "He called Beck, asked him to stop at the florist and find the best and biggest bouquet of yellow roses that he could find."

Chapter 46

Blair was on a hunt, the paper held in a shaking hand. He had just discovered something about Dan that he needed to talk with Neasa and Breck about and he could find neither one of them. It was the next day, and he was suddenly afraid.

Running for the outdoors, Blair searched the grounds, finding the couple in the gym, appearing to be at a stand-off over a treadmill. He paused, shaking his head before he hid his grin. Breck, Neasa is just what you need. She doesn't back down from you. It's not that you like your own way. It's just that you have a plan in mind when you approach people, sometimes not listening to us. Not that your plans are wrong. In fact, they usually work out for the best.

"Breck. Neasa. I need to speak with you two."

"Go away, Blair. We're in the middle of a huge fight." Neasa didn't look at him.

Breck stared at her. "You don't tell friends to leave. And we are not fighting. We are having a discussion."

"A fight. One that you seem determined to win. To have your own way. That's not how couples do it, Breck. We discuss, come to a compromise. What is so difficult about that? Have you never compromised in your life?"

"He has, Neasa. Let's set that aside. Neasa, I have new information about your parents."

"Which ones? The real ones? The step ones?" Neasa still did not look around.

"Your real ones. Neasa! Please!" Blair's tone of voice got through to her at last and she turned.

"What do you have?"

"This." He handed her the paper. "This is what I've found. Your parents weren't from here. Did you know that?"

"I knew Dan and his wife weren't. That he moved here to start his business. Pops mentioned that once and then shut right up. I think that they were scared of Dan."

"Scared that if they said anything, he would refuse to let you see them?" Breck reached for the paper, glancing over it. "They were from the other side of the province? Strange that they ended up here."

"She had connections. Neasa doesn't like to say her name, I can see that."

"No, I don't. As far as I'm concerned, she doesn't exist." Neasa stared at the two men. "What does that mean?" She stabbed a finger at the paper.

"It means that she is involved in something as well. Dan wasn't involved on his own. Dallas is working on this as well." Blair stabbed a finger at the door. "He was looking for you two a while ago."

Neasa walked away quickly, needing to get away from Breck. He's trying, Lord, isn't he? But trying too hard. I don't know which is worse. His not remembering or his trying to remember and driving me to distraction? Her steps slowed as she became lost in thought, jumping as she heard voices near her.

"Neasa?" Hagen stood near her, Guenivere and Jaxcy with her.

"Sorry. I was lost in thought, trying to sort out something. What can I do for you ladies?"

Jaxcy grinned. "We've all been there. Still are at times with our guys. We usually prepare meals when they're working like they are. Come. Join us. I talked to Bonnie earlier. She and Beck are heading home. They have to travel tomorrow."

"Oh, I missed her. I'm sorry." Neasa looked sad for a moment. "He's so lucky. To have a mother like Bonnie."

"We know, Neasa. We know." Jaxcy reached to hug her. "I thought mine were killed when I was seventeen. Only they were taken overseas and kept there. Friends found them and brought them back. We're still working through issues from that, but I am just so glad to have them back in my life. I'll share with you."

"She shares her parents with us, just like Cadee does. And have you seen Fynn's building of creepy-crawlies yet?" Guenivere linked her arm with Neasa. "If not, we are definitely planning a field trip."

"No, I haven't. I haven't been away from this building other than to church for days. I have no transportation." Neasa looked upset. "And I need to replace my bike,"

"You haven't?" Jaxcy shook her head. "That has to change. Let's get the fellows their meal and then we're going on a road trip with as many of the ladies as I can track down. The twins, too. And knowing Berneen's brother, Darbie? He'll want to come. He insists that we need a guy with us, as he puts it. I think he likes to shop, just doesn't want to admit to it."

Chapter 47

Standing outside late that afternoon, Breck rubbed at his head. He had a headache, he decided, and that he definitely didn't like. He also couldn't find Neasa. He had tapped at her door, without any response. In fact, he decided, he hadn't seen or heard from any of the ladies that afternoon.

Barnabas watched his friend, praying for him, asking for healing and a remembrance of his love for Neasa. For love her, he knew Breck did. He walked towards him.

"Breck? You've been standing here for ages."

"I know, Barnabas. I can't find Neasa. Dallas had word that Dan is actively searching for her."

"The ladies all headed into town, Darby and the twins with them. Jaxcy told me that Neasa needed it. She has not been away from here except for church."

Breck groaned, his eyes closing. "No, she has not. And we need to look for transportation for her." He looked around as he heard the sound of a motorcycle. "She didn't, did she?"

"I would say that she did. She needed to, Breck. She needs to reclaim her life and this is part of it. You didn't seem willing to help her, in her eyes. The ladies were." Barnabas' hand rested on his friend's shoulder for a moment. "She's fragile right now, Breck."

"I know. I just don't know what to say to her. It seems everything I say? We end up having words."

"Remember this. Tell her that you still want to go on a long ride with a beautiful lady. You told her that the morning you two left the hospital, way back at the beginning."

"I did?" Breck shook his head. "That's not me."

"Sorry, my friend. Where Neasa is concerned, it is. You are flirting with her more and more. Trust me on this. We all saw it and welcomed it for you. She's good for you." Barnabas waved as he walked away, surrounded suddenly by ladies.

Breck walked slowly towards where Neasa had parked her motorbike, not seeing the interest that she had attracted. Brendon, Brennen, and Brody watched from near the gym. He studied her as she slipped from the bike, reaching to rub the handlebar, and then stand back staring at it.

"You found a nice one, darling." Breck spoke from where he had stopped beside her.

"I did. It's a new year model but I got a really good deal on it. I know the owner. We went to school together. I don't think he made anything on it." She sniffed. "It's nice but it's not the same. I needed transportation, Breck."

"I know, darling. I know. I should have taken you, but I guess fear won."

"How can you say that? You don't remember me."

"I'm starting to, I think. Bits and pieces are starting to come through the thick head that Mom always says I have." Breck walked around the bike. "Does your friend have a matching one?"

"A matching one?" Neasa stared at him. "You want one?"

"I do. That way, we can go on rides together." Breck stood in front of her, his hands resting on her shoulders. "But in the meantime, you need transportation for winter."

"I do, but it doesn't matter." Neasa watched him. "We need to talk, Breck. I saw Dan in town. He and his wife. They're back together. I wonder if she even left town. He was watching the ladies. They tried to cover for me but some of them are so short. Darbie wouldn't leave my side. I can't have him hurt."

"That's Darbie. He's very protective of all the ladies here. Goes back to what happened with Berneen." Breck helped her to cover the motorcycle and then reached for her helmet and then her hand.

"Breck? What are you saying with this?" Neasa raised their joined hands.

"That I want to go on with what we had planned for our lives. I will remember, Neasa. That much I know. Right now, though? We need to keep you safe and solve whatever it is that Dan and his wife are involved with." He paused. "Do you think that she's the one behind it all?"

"Could be. Did you know that she has a sister?"

"She does? Is that the name they came up with?"

"I think it is. I never saw her that I remember. But I did see her name one day. I just need to remember it." Neasa frowned. "I don't know that I have ever said her name. It's Jessie."

"Jessie? I see. I think the fellows discovered that. They were being sensitive, not asking you." Breck held the door open. "And I have flowers for you. I didn't get a chance to give them to you."

Neasa grinned. "The best and biggest bouquet of yellow roses? Your mother squealed on you."

"She did, did she? She thinks of you as a daughter, Neasa, one that she could never have. She'll spoil you."

"Jessie's sister is Jane Light." Neasa's voice grew sad. "What did they take from us, Breck? And why?"

Chapter 48

Neasa stood by the restaurant door, watching as Breck ran back towards her, the cool rain pelting at his hooded jacket. He grinned at her as he shook his head.

"It's wet."

"Rain usually is." She walked into the restaurant entry, looking around. "I don't know that I have ever eaten in here. We never went out for meals."

"You didn't? That's strange." Breck lifted a hand to the waitress and pointed to a table near the back of the room.

Neasa shrugged. "It's who we were as a family. We hardly had any takeout either. They just never did that." She slipped from her coat, hanging it over the back of her chair, seating herself so that Breck could move her chair forward before he sat across from her.

"Don't worry about the cost, darling. Tonight, this is for you. As a thank you for being who you are."

She stared at Breck, not quite sure of what he was saying. "Breck?"

"I remember, darling, I remember."

"Oh, praise the Lord. I thought that I was going to have to hit you over the head or something."

Breck laughed at her even as he pointed to her menu. "And you would do just that, I know."

Later, walking back towards his truck, her hand in his, Neasa kept as close to Breck as she could.

"Breck, I'm scared." Neasa looked around the dimly lit parking lot.

"I know, darling. So am I." Breck tucked her into his truck and then ran for his side, climbing in and starting the vehicle. "We need to talk, Neasa. Not just about what we want, but what we have found. Dallas has been hard at work for the last couple of days. He needs to solve this, arrest who he has to, and then move back to town."

"I know." Neasa's voice was barely a whisper. "I hate that he is giving up his life for us."

"He's okay with that. He has tracked down Jessie's sister. She was horrified to hear what Jessie had done. She lost track of her after your own father died and she moved away."

"What else? I hear the "but" in that sentence."

"There is. Dallas wasn't comfortable with some of what she said. He's speaking with someone on that city's police force." Breck drove away, watching carefully, not seeing the vehicle following him.

"What can we do for him, Breck? I don't know him that well, but he seems at odds with himself."

"That's a good way to put it. He is at odds with himself." Breck turned onto the road leading to the Foundation lands. "Some of us think that he'll resign shortly from the force and move on to something else."

Neasa nodded, her eyes on the road ahead of her. "Breck? What's on the road?"

Breck slowed and then stopped, reaching to ensure that the doors were locked. "I don't know, darling. But we're not getting out to find out. Call it in, will you?"

Neasa reached for her phone, a scream rising from her as she saw the man appear at her window. "Breck!"

Breck sat, his hands tense on the wheel, his mind racing as to how to get them out of there. He watched as the man hammered at Neasa's window, Neasa shrinking back from it.

"Neasa? Your seatbelt it tight?"

"It is. You're planning something."

"I am. I think that's just a wooden barricade. I'm going to try and ram it, to see if I can get through it. Someone has moved in behind us."

"Great. We go out for dinner and then get into danger. What next?" Neasa's fingers whitened as she tightened her hold on her seatbelt. "I would say, go for it, but it's your truck, Breck."

"Which can be replaced. You can't." Breck sent up a quick prayer and then gunned the motor, not seeing anyone in front of him. Wood flew from where he rammed the barricade, the truck sliding on the wet road before he straightened it and sped down the road, barely slowing to turn into the Foundation gate. He parked quickly, reached to lift Neasa over the console and out of his side of the truck, and then ran for the back entrance, which was the nearest. He keyed in the combination and pulled the door open, shoving her through.

Neasa stared at him in shock and disbelief.

"Did we really just do that?"

"We did. Hurry. Up to your apartment. I need you safe." Breck pulled her with him towards the stairs, hesitating for a moment. "No, I think my office." He headed that way, the door unlocked, and then shoved shut and locked behind them. He walked carefully through the office before he reached to turn on a light at the reception desk.

"Breck?" Neasa stood in front of him, arms crossed. "Why not my apartment?"

He shrugged. "Something told me not to. I have learned to listen to God when He tells me things like that."

Chapter 49

Breck paced his office, watching Neasa closely as she sat at the reception desk, her hands busy with the mail that sat there. He had protested but she had ignored him, continuing on with what she was doing, rising at one point to head for his office, laying down a number of letters that he needed to look at. He finally shook his head and continued to pace.

Hearing a tap at the door, he raised his hand to Neasa, who nodded, moving on silent feet to stand with his ear to it. The tap came again, this time with a voice calling his name. He reached to unlock the door and Dallas and Barnabas slipped in.

"What did you go and do, Breck?" Dallas looked angry.

"Just ran a barricade. What was that all about?"

Dallas turned as Neasa approached, to be swept close to Breck. "They were waiting for you, Breck. Officers were following you and before they could get to the situation, you have moved through it. They were to take you captive and take you away."

"We gathered that. Who?" Breck's arm tightened around Neasa."

"Her step-father, Dan. The men here heard something around your apartment. They were waiting up there for you as well. We have those ones in custody."

"How did they get in?" Breck was puzzled. "Our security is good."

"They slipped in by the looks of it on the video feed when Jack was out on his rounds. They are keeping that close an eye on here." Barnabas was both angry and frustrated.

"That close?" Neasa's hand grasped for Breck. "Breck wouldn't let us go upstairs. Why not wait down here?"

"Because they are not likely sure which is his office. They have figured out the apartments here and I would like to know how." Dallas paced. "Did you see anything off when you were out tonight?"

Breck shook his head. "Not a thing. And I was watching. Even in the restaurant. I took our favourite table, at the back, near the kitchen."

"And the staff knows us well enough to say something, if they saw anything." Barnabas paced. "The fellows are pulling an all-nighter, Breck. They are close to finding all the information. Emma has been silent, which isn't like her."

"No, it isn't. I had an email from her this morning. Abe and his team were called away suddenly on an assignment. She was called away with them."

"That explains it." Barnabas turned suddenly to Neasa. "Neasa? What can we do for you?"

"I have no idea, Barnabas. I never thought of that." She paused. "My Pops and Grams? How safe are they?"

Barnabas grinned. "We thought of that, Neasa. Andy, Brennen, and Jaxcy flew up there tonight. They're going to try and persuade them to move this way, or at least come for a visit."

"They are? Oh, that would be wonderful. I have been so scared for them."

"And you never said a word." Breck hugged her. "You need to talk to us, darling, but I know it's difficult, given what you've not said about your life."

Neasa smacked him before she moved away, fatigue suddenly weighing at her.

"How long?"

Dallas stared at her, a puzzled look on his face. "How long?"

"Right. How long before I can go home? Not that I object to your company, but sometimes a gal just needs to be by herself."

Dallas laughed, knowing exactly what she was doing. "Soon. The team is going through the hallway and the stairs, and then you'll be able to go home. I'm sorry, Neasa. Sorry that you had to face this after your date with Breck."

Neasa shrugged. "It's what I've come to expect. He seems to like danger."

"Me? Like danger? I thought you were the one who liked danger." Breck protested, knowing that was what she expected.

Barnabas stared at the three in the room with him before he too laughed. "Neasa, you are exactly what we need in this building. The other ladies have brought laughter and fun, but you add just that certain touch, like the right spice or seasoning, to our family. Have you two set a date yet?"

"A date? I thought that was what we just had." She smirked at Barnabas as he stared at her before she winked.

"No, we have not set a date, but I think we will. Let's get her grandparents here." Breck had a thought. "Her mother's family?"

"We've looked, Neasa. Brody has made this his mission. He is on the track of a cousin, he said, but he can't find any living relations. He says it looks as if your mother was an orphan when she married your father, with a brother who had married and moved out west."

"A cousin? Oh, that would be wonderful. Nevin and I were always envious of those who had cousins."

Chapter 50

The next morning, Breck stood in the conference room, watching as the fellows dished up plates of food and then gathered around tables set apart from their work stations, their ladies with them. Neasa stood beside him, her hand tight in his. She was envious, for a moment, of the fact that the couples were married and didn't have to stay apart. She had wanted to be with Breck last night, just to be held in his arms and prayed for.

Breck's hand tightened on hers before he spoke.

"Neasa, we need to eat, but first, I need to ask you a question."

"The answer is yes. A week from Saturday works."

He stared at her. "Neasa? You didn't even know what I was going to ask."

"I did, Breck, because you want the same thing. You don't want an apartment wall between us, not when you're that concerned and frightened for me." She looked up at him, her love for him on her face. "Why should we wait? Nevin has said for us to go ahead, as much as he would want to be here."

"He did?"

"He did. I spent an hour on the phone with him last night, going over everything, just touching base.

He would be saddened not to be here, but he wants us to go ahead.”

“If we could get them back to the building, they could be here.”

“True, but I won’t put them at risk.” She looked up at him again. “Ask your question.”

“Neasa, will you marry me a week from Saturday?”

“I will.”

Breck bent to kiss her and then looked over at the men. “I wonder if Buckley is free then. Did I ever tell you that he offered dates to two of the couples, not thinking that they would take him up on them?”

“I hope that they did. It would serve him right. He’s serious and all but does like to tease and torment, as Grams would say.”

“He does.” Breck held their plates as she dished them up before she reached for their drinks and then headed to the tables, sitting in the spots saved for them.

Buckley watched them for a while before he spoke up.

“Listen, you two. I have a week from Saturday open, in case you want to set a date. Unless you want Daniel to do the honours.”

Breck shared a look with Neasa before he too spoke.

“Quite the coincidence. We were planning on that date.”

The men and ladies broke out into laughter and then talk even as Buckley shook his head.

"Got me again, didn't you?"

"We did." Breck smirked before he sobered. "We would like to try and bring Nevin and Sarah back if we can arrange that."

"We should be able to. Barnabas?" Brady looked towards him.

"I think it's time they came home anyway. Dallas is needing to spend more time speaking with him and is finding it difficult over the phone." Barnabas excused himself as he pulled out his phone. "Sorry, people. I need to take this."

"One thing that I don't understand." Benen spoke up. "You two aren't getting the text messages, the letters, the photos, the packages, the threats that we all did."

"No, we aren't." Breck shared a look with Neasa. "And that has puzzled us as well. It's as if they aren't really trying anymore. Does that mean whoever it is has moved on?"

"Or are they planning one last grand stand?" Bradon looked down at Ennis. "We've talked about that. I think they are going to make one last play and that will be the most dangerous one. Even that bit on the road? It was poorly set up. With two guys? Who does that?"

"Dan does." Neasa finally spoke. "It's the way he would work. I have watched his work over the years. He just finds the minimum that he needs. Even with the work on the playground? Nevin and I should not have been the ones. He had others that were more experienced. He used the excuse that we needed the experience, that we liked to play in the dirt." She shuddered for a moment. "I mean, I liked working the equipment, Nevin liked setting it all up, but it's not what we were used to. Nevin was the one who found the work for us, did the contracts, all the contacts. I was the one who sourced material and greenery and plants. Why put us out there like that on that particular day?"

Burnie pointed at her. "That what we want to know. He had to have known that we would find bones when we started that dig. So why you two?"

"I think it was a psychological way of keeping control of the two." Fynn spoke up. "I have seen it before. If he had used the other men, it would not have affected them the same way. Digging up their father? How has that affected Neasa and Nevin? He knew it would. He thought that he could keep control of them by using that. Instead, Breck stepped in with Neasa. Nevin walked away with Sarah. That left him without anyone. He's angry and will come after you again, Breck and Neasa. And there is someone behind him. We all know that. Who owned the property before the Foundation?"

Chapter 51

Barnabas had stood, listening to Fynn speak, before he left the room, heading for his office. His father would know who that was.

"Dad?" Barnabas spoke to his father even as he searched his filing cabinet. "The shelter? Do you remember who owned that property?"

"I do. John and I were going over that the night before last. Your mother and I are heading your way, this time for good, son."

"You are? Oh, that's wonderful, Dad. I will be glad to have you back in town. What brought that on?"

"Your mother wants to. We've sold our property here just yesterday. It's time, son. We're not getting any younger. She doesn't want to travel as much as we have been for the Foundation. I agree. It's time to let someone else take over that."

"I don't want it, Dad. I like what I do."

"We know you do. We have someone in mind, the board and I. We're in talks with this young man. But you called. What was that about the shelter?"

"Fynn asked who owned it before we acquired it."

"That would have been Larry Light. Why?"

"Because Neasa said that she and Nevin should not have been the ones working that day. That Dan had others who were more experienced. Fynn made the observation that it would have been to keep control of the siblings.”

“And from what I understand and can remember of Dan, that would have been it. I mean, we’re friends, but there has always been something hidden, we felt, that he didn’t want anyone to know about. This is likely it.”

“It is. I’m glad you’re heading here. When do you leave?”

“The movers come in on Monday. Your mother is leaving everything to them, other than our personal things. We’ll head out Tuesday morning and be there that night.”

“Good. Breck and Neasa have set a date for a week from Saturday. Breck would want you there. His parents are here, so that solves that.”

“Her brother?”

“We’ll bring them back next week. Andy is heading up to bring her grandparents here.”

“They have a farm?”

“They do. Neasa mentioned that it was almost too much for him over the past summer.”

“Okay. I’ll speak to him. The board is looking for something like that, to set up for men or couples who want to work outdoors and want to do that. This may be the opportunity we need.”

Barnabas headed back for the conference room, satisfied with his conversation. He paused just inside the doorway, watching as Neasa stood in front of Baird, tension radiating from her, Breck's arms around her.

"Baird?"

"Barnabas? Neasa remembered something, and she's not sharing. We think that she should."

"Neasa?" Barnabas' quiet voice turned her head towards him, and he drew in a deep breath at the devastation that showed.

"I remembered, Barnabas. Oh, how I wish I hadn't!"

"What did you remember, darling?" Breck's voice whispered in her ear.

"The land for the shelter? I can remember years ago, Dan and Jessie talking about it. Her brother-in-law owned it. Was he a part of this?"

"That's what we think, Neasa. I just spoke with Dad. He named a Larry Light." Barnabas shared a look with Breck. "He was involved in a suspected drunk driving accident years ago, but there was always a question about that. He didn't drink, but his blood-alcohol level was over the limit."

Dallas spoke from where he sat. "I'm looking into that, Breck. We don't have a lot of information, but we're going back through what we have. His name has come up a lot in these investigations. Will cleared it for me to talk to you about."

Neasa nodded. "What or who has Dan not touched and contaminated?"

Chapter 52

Breck and Neasa headed out the next morning, intent on living their lives. Neasa wanted to look at cars, and Breck had insisted that he take her. He had laughed when she had grumbled at him, saying he just wanted to find a matching bike to hers. He had kissed her and then led her from the building.

Their walk towards his truck stopped quickly as they saw the men waiting for them. Breck took a step backward, stopping as he felt something poke him in the back. He felt Neasa move closer to him and his hand tightened on hers.

"Just what we need, Breck. Dan and his henchman." Neasa's sarcasm came through as she spoke, her eyes on her step-father as he walked to stand directly in front of her.

Breck shot a look around, wondering that no one was outside. That was unusual for a Saturday morning. He was glad the ladies weren't, but where was security?

"You're coming with me, Neasa. This man isn't."

"No, I don't think so, Dan. You can't tell me what to do, not anymore. You haven't had that right in years, I might say, all my life. Did you kill Dad?"

"I'm your father." His hand was up, striking her across the face, a cut appearing on her lip.

Breck growled in rage and tried to reach for him, finding his arms tight to his body from the binding that had appeared from the men behind him. He struggled, finding Neasa torn from him. He lurched to the side, taking the man holding him off balance, and he freed his arms, charging towards Dan. A savage blow from the side stopped him in his tracks and then dropped him to the cold pavement, his vision darkening and then fading.

Neasa screamed, trying her best to wrench herself from Dan's grip, not able to as he pulled her towards a vehicle.

"I'm not going with you!" Her voice was loud in the sudden silence. She thought that she saw movement off to one side, but didn't dare look. "You've hurt someone I love for the last time." Her hand was up, her nails clawing at his face, her fingers poking at his eyes.

A cry of hurt and then rage came from him as he dropped her arm to cover his face. She was on her hands and knees and then her feet, scrambling away from the men, heading towards cover, she prayed. A hand over her mouth stifled her scream and then she heard Brendon's voice in her ear.

"We've got you, Neasa. We have help on the way, but they won't make it in time. Here, in you go to the building. Head for the conference room and lock the door. The ladies are waiting for you." Brendon shoved at her as she hesitated. "Go. We'll get Breck and bring him to you."

Neasa ran down the hallway, her breath catching in her throat, fear lending speed to her feet. She flew through the doorway, slamming it behind her and locking it, standing staring at the ladies, a hand on her throat, her breath coming in gasps.

"How did you know?"

"Security saw them moving in. He couldn't get to you two, so he came here." Fynn was angry. "Our guys are out there, and we're stuck in here."

"We are but what can we do?" Hagen looked around, her eyes on her sisters who held her son and daughter. "I, for one, am tired of them bringing the fight to our home. What can we do, ladies? I'm not standing back. Not anymore. Breck has helped too many of us."

"He has." Berneen moved towards the door. "You know, there are fire hoses outside the building. We could always turn them on."

"Don't we need a key to do that?"

Berneen shook her head. "No. That is one thing that is not locked down. Who's with me? Other than the ones who are pregnant? You stay put."

"That makes most of us. Let's go, ladies." Cadee turned to Berneen. "You shouldn't be going."

"It was my idea. Of course, I'm going." She was out of the door, walking as quickly and as quietly as she could for the outside. The other ladies followed, leaving the two girls to lock themselves in.

Half of the ladies went to one side of the building, the other seven to the other side, Neasa in front, reaching for the hose and unrolling it as she crept towards the front, to stand peeking around the corner at the standoff in the parking lot. Berneen peeked around as well.

"A stand-off. And Breck is still down and out. Or is he?"

"No, he's awake. Just playing possum as they say." Neasa watched Breck intently. "He's hurting."

"He is." Berneen moved backward, whispering quietly to the other ladies, who nodded. Hands on the hose, they were ready, one standing back by the valve, ready to turn the water on.

Chapter 53

Barnabas stood where Dan could see him, the other men standing in a loose circle around the intruders. He didn't dare make more of a move, not with one of the intruders holding a revolver pointing directly at Breck's head. Any move might just cause that to go off. He frowned for a moment as he saw Breck's eyes open and a slight nod from him. Okay, Barnabas thought, he's ready to move when we do. Lord, this is where it gets hard. Any false move might just get my friend killed. Give us the strength and wisdom that we need.

Dallas watched from where he had taken a position behind Dan, his revolver out and down at his side. He was ready, but he didn't watch to use it, just in case one of the Foundation men were hurt. Lord, he prayed as well, guide our words and our actions.

Baird was standing where he could see the end of the building and frowned. Berneen? Neasa? I thought you were told to stay locked away. What are you planning? He frowned deeper and then a smile flickered across his face as he saw Cadee and Ennis peeking around the other corner. He caught a glimpse of the fire hoses in the ladies' hand. Lord, protect these ladies. They're trying to help. Don't let any one of them be hurt.

Dan began to pace. This was not going as he had planned. Neasa and Breck were to have cooperated with him and gone into the vehicle. That they wouldn't have never crossed his mind. Neasa had always done what he had demanded. She had changed, and that man had done it. It didn't occur to him that Neasa had come to understand just who he himself was and his character and had decided that she had had enough.

His men shifted on their feet, not liking that they were out in the open and surrounded as they were. They had the weapons, those men didn't, they all thought, but without Dan's direction, they couldn't use them. He had made that abundantly clear. If one did, they would all pay the price. And they all knew the price that he would demand.

Baird's eyes flickered to the ladies once more and then his ear caught the sound of vehicles slowing and stopping on the road. Help or not, he wondered. He glanced around, seeing the other men had also heard them. He watched Dallas for a moment as he felt for his phone on the holster attached to his belt and then nodded. Good, Friends. Now to stall this until they walked up and surrounded the men.

Dan's attention went to the road and he began to yell, his words unintelligible. He stalked towards Breck, his arms waving before a boot was out and he kicked Breck, sending him rolling away from him and more towards the building. The man who had been covering him stood where he was, not moving, his eyes on Dan.

The building men looked up as they heard female shouts and then dropped to the ground as the force of the water from the fire hoses hit Dan and his men. The ladies struggled to control the hoses, their feet digging into the ground, even as some of the men were on their feet, heading to help them. Dan and his men floundered on the ground as the force of the water kept them down and out of the way. The officers who had responded moved in, once the water was turned off, handcuffing the men, reading them their rights, and then hustling the soaking wet men away, smiles and nods directed to the ladies.

Dallas stood in awe as he watched the women run for their men, to be swept into hard hugs. Neasa was on her knees, her arms around Breck as he sat up with Brady's help, almost knocking him back down from how hard she hit him as her arms surrounding him.

"Breck? You're hurt. Did he hurt you?" Neasa's words tumbled over one another, not letting Breck say anything. Baird was on his feet, heading for where Berneen stood.

"You ladies did good, my love. But weren't you supposed to stay in the conference room?" Baird hugged her hard before he kissed her.

"We were, but we couldn't. We had to help. Breck was there for all of us." Berneen was close to tears.

"I know, my love. I know. He'll tell you off, you know."

Berneen peeked around Baird and grinned. "Somehow, I don't think he will."

Breck finally just swept Neasa close and kissed her thoroughly. It was the only way that he could stop her words.

"You're not hurt, darling?" He searched her face.

"No, he just made me angry. The hoses worked well, I think."

Breck began to laugh. "They worked extremely well. I'm proud of you and all the ladies. You stepped in with a solution that the men didn't think of."

"Of course, we did. Our brains work differently than men's do." Neasa smirked at him. "Now, it is over? Can we start living once more?"

Dallas crouched down beside them. "You're okay, Breck? You took a good hit."

"I'm okay. I saw it coming and rolled before he really touched me. The other blow? Nothing more than I've had playing football and been tackled." Breck took Dallas' outstretched hand to help him stand, Neasa back in his arms as he did so.

"I think that it's over, Neasa. We have everyone. I had just received word that Larry Light, his wife, and your step-mother were all arrested this morning. They were looking for Dan when he showed up here. Give us a few days, and then we'll meet to discuss what we can." He waved as he headed for his car, intent on questioning the men and women involved in all this.

Barnabas walked towards Breck, his eyes assessing his friend.

"Okay, friend?"

"I am, Barnabas. Thanks to the ladies, and to you fellows as well, I can say that. Dallas let us know that they have made the arrests that they needed to."

"Good. Now, let's get you both inside. Breck, you need some dry clothes. I don't think that you expected to take a shower out here. Give us a couple of hours and we'll meet in the chapel this afternoon."

Chapter 54

Four days later, Dallas appeared in the conference room, finding all the men and ladies waiting for him. He stood for a moment, eyeing them all, before he found Breck and Neasa, sitting off in a corner, arms around one another, heads together as they prayed. He hesitated to talk towards them but did as their heads raised. Breck was on his feet, a hand out to shake Dallas'.

"Dallas. Thank you for what you have done. I know that you've been struggling lately."

"I have been, Breck. Not related to what you have gone through. Neasa? You're okay?"

Neasa was on her feet, hugging Dallas, able only to whisper a thank you in his ear.

"You have news, Dallas?" Breck had caught the movement of the others as they found seats and were watching them.

"I do. I think it's going to be easier for you to accept, Neasa, than I expected it to be. Your brother and wife are here?"

"They are, as are our grandparents. The fellows tracked down a cousin, but he wasn't really interested in hearing from us."

"I'm sorry. That happens, but it doesn't make it any easier. Shall we?"

Breck nodded, his eyes searching for Buckley, who nodded and stood, his prayer echoing through the room.

"Thank you, Buckley. Dallas, the floor is yours." Breck moved Neasa to sit at one of the tables, reaching for the pen and paper as he always did. It was a force of habit that he just could not give up.

"Thanks, Breck. And thank you, Buckley, for your prayers. And each one of you fellows and your ladies? Once more, you have found the information far more quickly than we could. Emma hasn't been able to help this time, she said, not like she wanted to. Circumstances altered that for her. She sends her thanks as well." He paused, his eyes find the grandparents, then Nevin and Sarah, and finally Breck and his lady, Neasa. Lord, she is well. They both survived. They are in love and heading for a wedding this Saturday. Thank you, Lord, for protecting this friend of ours, who is so needed in this family. His quiet words and prayers and care and concern keep us all in touch with You and learning more and more how to love You more and each other better.

"Neasa, Nevin? I have spoken intensely with Dan. He finally admitted that it was his fault that your father was killed. He had approached him about coming into partnership with your father in his landscaping business. Your father had refused. Dan grew angry and shoved him, causing him to fall. Your grandparents did let us know that your father had a heart condition. What the medical examiner thinks happened is that with the fall, your father had a heart attack and didn't survive. Dan has admitted that your father seemed to be in distress but that he had walked away to cool off. When he returned, he panicked as your father had died. He buried him on the land that Larry Light had, using that as leverage against Light. Light has been involved in shady deals, as they are sometimes called, substandard work and blackmail. Dan knew this and used it against him as well.

"Light has admitted to all of this and much more. His wife was pushing him to leave the area and he sold out to the Foundation, not telling them of the body buried there. They moved away. He returned voluntarily to face the charges against him.

"Your step-mother? She is something else. She knew what had happened to your father, married Dan, and then threatened to turn him in. He was abusive to her all their marriage. She did put in complaints and then withdrew them. She has admitted to another detective that she married your father in haste and regretted it. She didn't want to raise someone else's kids, as she put it. She has stated that she was heading for a divorce when he died. She didn't feel that she could place you children into care and refused to let your grandparents have you."

"Who ran us down?" Breck looked over at Dallas as he asked that.

"We never found out who that was. Dan, if he knows, isn't saying." Dallas looked apologetic.

Neasa nodded. "Somehow, that's what I thought you would say. It's all over?"

"It is, Neasa. A bad choice that led to death and then cover up. You, Nevin, and your grandparents paid the price for years because of that. Now, you can heal. God will lead you in that." Dallas closed his portfolio and simply walked away. He was tired, Lord, he thought. Tired and burnt out. I need a change. Maybe that job offer that came out of nowhere? That might just be where You want me.

That next Saturday, Barnabas stood and watched the building family as they mingled and laughed and teased one another. *It has grown, Lord, from just Doc and Anna and myself as each one of the men appeared and joined it. Then, the ladies joined, some with siblings, and some with parents, and one with a Granny, and now Neasa with her Pops and Grams. We are blessed with each one.* He sought out his parents, who stood talking with Neasa's grandparents and Breck's parents.

He then sought out Breck and Neasa, who stood, arms around one another, clearly in love, as they took the good-natured teasing that he had come to expect from the men and the ladies as well. *Neasa was fitting in,* he thought. *She is exactly who Breck has needed. He likes to tease but has a heart of gold. She has a dry sense of humour that completes his. She is already taking care of the ladies, without realizing that she is.*

Breck finally made his way to where Barnabas stood, handing him a mug of coffee and then just standing by his friend. *They had been friends since toddles,* he thought, *having their disagreements but standing shoulder to shoulder with one another when needed.*

"Barnabas? What can I say? We've been friends for so many years, but that's changing now."

"It is, my friend, but it is right and proper. We'll remain friends, but that lady there? She becomes your best friend and confidant. I understand. God brought a very special lady into your life."

Breck grinned. "He did. I pray that you find your lady, Barnabas. We all do."

Barnabas shrugged. "I'm sure that if she's out there, He will lead me to her. You're away for what, two weeks?"

"We are. And you head out that day. You need the break, Barnabas. What's happened with all the men has weighed you down."

"It has, but God has provided for us all." He grinned as he watched the ladies hovering over the little ones. "With the little ones coming now, we need to do some planning for safe spots for them."

"And we will. Nevin has taken over the company that Dan had and his first work will be the shelter and then he's moving in here, he tells me, to do a playground and fenced area for the little ones."

"He is?" Barnabas wasn't surprised. "That he will. He's part of our family." He grew quiet, sipping at his coffee, even as he watched the men and ladies. "How's Neasa after all this?"

"Hurting, as you can imagine. Questioning. Searching for answers. Have her grandparents here will help. And with Nevin and Sarah back, she has someone who lived it with her that she can talk to."

"That she does. She has a huge heart, under all her fun and teasing. And she wants to share it with the ones in the building. She told me that she didn't realize that marrying you meant that she would take on such a role."

"She knows that but wants to. She's also volunteering at the shelter to teach simple cooking classes when we can get that going." Breck reached out an arm to wrap around Neasa as she approached.

"Thank you, Barnabas, for this. I didn't expect it."

Barnabas just grinned and shrugged. "The board wanted to do it for you both. You're an important part of our family. Dad says that he wants to talk with you more about your work, but there is no pressure on that. He wants your input on what you see here."

"And I will gladly give it." She tilted her head to look at him. "You're hurting, Barnabas. I hear you're on vacation when we come back. Find your lady, bring her home with you."

Barnabas stared at her for a moment before he hugged her and walked away, his mug placed carefully on the table before he left the room.

Neasa watched him walk away before she looked up at Breck. "Breck?"

"You didn't say anything wrong, Neasa. He's been hurting for a while. We've all seen it. None of us have figured it out. The ladies have suggested that he's hurting for someone who walked away from him. Honestly? I don't remember him showing interest in anyone since we were in college. There was a lady then, but I don't seem to remember it being serious."

"It could have been serious, but they kept it on the light side for some reason." Neasa turned in his arms. "We are blessed with many friends, sweetheart."

"We are, my darling. That we are. Have I told you today that I love you?"

Neasa nodded, a smile on her lips as she did so. "You have, but not enough." Her head turned up for his kiss. "Hmm. I think I like this. You're a keeper."

Breck broke out into laughter, bringing eyes to them, before he spoke.

"Neasa, you do my heart good. You tell me that I have taught you to love. You have done the same for me. You have taught me to love God more and more each day. You have taught me to love you and that too grows more and more every minute I'm around you and when I'm not. Your reaction to the ones who wronged you has shown me that we can love them too, even when they plot evil for us. Thank you, my love."

"And you have taught me as well." She reached to kiss him. "Thank you for being the man of God that you are. Grams and Pops have both told me that you are what they prayed for, just for me. Sarah is Nevin's heart."

"That they are." Breck reached for her hand. "We need to mingle, my love, and I understand that there is a cake to cut." He twirled her around, studying the simple white, lace-covered dress that she had chosen, and the yellow roses that he had given her in her hair. "You are just so beautiful today."

———

Thank you for picking up the story of Breck and his love, Neasa. This was quite the story, not like the others but similar in ways. She was not what I expected for him, not at all. She kept rebelling about her name, finally letting me settle on Neasa. To have her riding a motorcycle? Nope, not planned at all, but it fit her personality.

As always, the characters have driven the story. I might want it to go one way but the unruly characters take over and don't share the road map or the GPS coordinators. It is always interesting and a challenge to follow where they lead.

How do we love? How do we teach someone to love? It's hard, particularly in these days when anger and hate seem to prevalent. I look to Christ. How did He teach this? First, by example. Second, by His words. We can follow no one better than our Lord in teaching or learning love.

The folks from *His Guardians* only came in by name this time. They didn't walk in and out of this story. Emma and Abe are in this series. Darcie's story is *The Heart of a Lion.*

God bless each one of you as you walk with Him. Even in the times that we are living, with the restrictions of the COVID-19 virus that is prevalent world wife, He is there with each of us, in every way.

Ronna

www.ingramcontent.com/pod-product-compliance
Lightning Source LLC
Chambersburg PA
CBHW061240210726
48293CB00003B/840